It promised to be a busy week for the Flaxbor-ough constabulary. A bumbling inquiry agent imported from London was hot on the heels of an adulterer. A rash of white-collar crime had erupted among the area's charitable organiza-tions—of which a full thirty-six were devoted to saving our four-footed friends. And to top it all off, an anonymous letter written by a fright-ened woman had arrived—predicting her immi-nent death and holding no clue to her identity.

It was a perplexing predicament for Detective Inspector Purbright until a matronly do-gooder turned up facedown in the water of a Styrofoam wishing well. Then he began to piece together an intriguing puzzle of good deeds and foul play, enabling him to corner a killer who thought he was too clever to give himself away.

Murder Ink.® Mysteries

1   DEATH IN THE MORNING, Sheila Radley

3   THE BRANDENBURG HOTEL, Pauline Glen Winslow

5   McGARR AND THE SIENESE CONSPIRACY,
Bartholomew Gill

7   THE RED HOUSE MYSTERY, A. A. Milne

9   THE MINUTEMAN MURDERS, Jane Langton

11   MY FOE OUTSTRETCH'D BENEATH THE TREE,
V. C. Clinton-Baddeley

13   GUILT EDGED, W. J. Burley

15   COPPER GOLD, Pauline Glen Winslow

17   MANY DEADLY RETURNS, Patricia Moyes

19   McGARR AT THE DUBLIN HORSE SHOW,
Bartholomew Gill

21   DEATH AND LETTERS, Elizabeth Daly

23   ONLY A MATTER OF TIME, V. C. Clinton-Baddeley

25   WYCLIFFE AND THE PEA-GREEN BOAT,
W. J. Burley

27   ANY SHAPE OR FORM, Elizabeth Daly

29   COFFIN SCARCELY USED, Colin Watson

31   THE CHIEF INSPECTOR'S DAUGHTER,
Sheila Radley

33   PREMEDICATED MURDER, Douglas Clark

35   NO CASE FOR THE POLICE, V. C. Clinton-Baddeley

37   JUST WHAT THE DOCTOR ORDERED,
Colin Watson

39   DANGEROUS DAVIES, Leslie Thomas

41   THE GIMMEL FLASK, Douglas Clark

43   SERVICE OF ALL THE DEAD, Colin Dexter

45   DEATH'S BRIGHT DART, V. C. Clinton-Baddeley

47   GOLDEN RAIN, Douglas Clark

49   THE MAN WITH A LOAD OF MISCHIEF,
Martha Grimes

51   DOWN AMONG THE DEAD MEN, Patricia Moyes

53   HOPJOY WAS HERE, Colin Watson

55   NIGHT WALK, Elizabeth Daly

57   SITUATION TRAGEDY, Simon Brett

59   CHARITY ENDS AT HOME, Colin Watson

Scene Of The Crime® Mysteries

2   A MEDIUM FOR MURDER, Mignon Warner

4   DEATH OF A MYSTERY WRITER, Robert Barnard

6   DEATH AFTER BREAKFAST, Hugh Pentecost

8   THE POISONED CHOCOLATES CASE,
Anthony Berkeley

10   A SPRIG OF SEA LAVENDER, J.R.L. Anderson

12   WATSON'S CHOICE, Gladys Mitchell

14   SPENCE AND THE HOLIDAY MURDERS,
Michael Allen

16   THE TAROT MURDERS, Mignon Warner

18   DEATH ON THE HIGH C's, Robert Barnard

20   WINKING AT THE BRIM, Gladys Mitchell

22   TRIAL AND ERROR, Anthony Berkeley

24   RANDOM KILLER, Hugh Pentecost

26   SPENCE AT THE BLUE BAZAAR, Michael Allen

28   GENTLY WITH THE INNOCENTS, Alan Hunter

30   THE JUDAS PAIR, Jonathan Gash

32   DEATH OF A LITERARY WIDOW,
Robert Barnard

34   THE TWELVE DEATHS OF CHRISTMAS,
Marian Babson

36   GOLD BY GEMINI, Jonathan Gash

38   LANDED GENTLY, Alan Hunter

40   MURDER, MURDER, LITTLE STAR, Marian Babson

42   DEATH IN A COLD CLIMATE, Robert Barnard

44   A CHILD'S GARDEN OF DEATH, Richard Forrest

46   GENTLY THROUGH THE WOODS, Alan Hunter

48   THE GRAIL TREE, Jonathan Gash

50   RULING PASSION, Reginald Hill

52   DEATH OF A PERFECT MOTHER, Robert Barnard

54   A COFFIN FROM THE PAST, Gwendoline Butler

56   AND ONE FOR THE DEAD, Pierre Audemars

58   DEATH ON THE HEATH, Alan Hunter

A Murder Ink® Mystery

CHARITY ENDS AT HOME

Colin Watson

A DELL BOOK

Published by
Dell Publishing Co., Inc.
1 Dag Hammarskjold Plaza
New York, New York 10017

Dell ® TM 681510, Dell Publishing Co., Inc.

ISBN: 0-440-11187-0

Reprinted by arrangement with the author
Printed in the United States of America
First Dell printing—April 1983

1

ONE of the most notable examples of what a former mayor of Flaxborough described with unconscious felicity as "the venereal institutions of this ancient town" was its coroner, Mr. Albert Amblesby.

He had endured in his office through four reigns. Only the oldest citizens could recall his appointment. It had been canvassed as a political favor by a group of local dignitaries whose affairs during the First World War had prospered through the shrewd advice of the junior partner in the firm of Sparrow, Sparrow and Amblesby, solicitors. What the advice had been, there was now no means of learning. The beneficiaries had long since departed, as had murmurous, lugubrious lawyer Sparrow and his dim brother. Even rumor, once pungent with questions about fraudulent cattle-feed contracts, selection-board bribes and a military highway that got no farther than the wharves of the Flaxborough Docking Company, had thinned and dissipated on the wind of time. As for Albert Amblesby himself, he had forgotten the circumstances of his preferment, together with many, many other things. His only certain knowledge was that he was clever enough to have awakened that morning to the lovely discovery that one person on whom no inquest could yet be called was Her Majesty's Coroner for Flaxborough and District.

Survival was the central fact and chief joy in the life of Mr. Amblesby. It was a triumph of which he was perpetually conscious. The deaths, one by one, of his partners, his wife, his old political cronies and, best of all, his enemies had been as gratifying as the salutes of guns in the ears of a tenacious old fortress commander.

Those who interpreted this attitude as callousness did Mr. Amblesby less than justice. He begrudged life to no one. He certainly had never wished anybody dead. But his firm and uncomplicated belief was that survival, like success in business, was purely a matter of personal acumen.

It was natural, then, that the Flaxborough coroner should conduct the functions of his office with neither sentimentality nor gloom. He presided over an inquest with a certain sardonic sharpness admirably calculated to save the bereaved relatives from the embarrassment of that public display of emotion which a kind word can so easily unloose. It was rather as if the affairs of the deceased had come under the scrutiny of an official receiver, prepared at the slightest sign of careless bookkeeping to order the corpse alive again to show cause why it should not be committed for contempt.

Sergeant Malley, the coroner's officer, would always privately warn witnesses that they might find Mr. Amblesby's bearing somewhat lacking in sympathy. "He doesn't mean any harm, really," he would tell them. "It's just that he's getting on a bit. You mustn't take notice of everything he says—he's a wonderful old gentleman for his age."

The sergeant's private and carefully guarded opinion was that the coroner was "a wicked old sod and a damned disgrace." Malley was a heavy, contemplative, wry-humored, patient man. His authority, such as it was, troubled and even shamed him. Who was he—who was anybody—to order other human beings around? They had grief enough without being bullied and badgered by senile inquisitors and their jacks-in-office.

One day in late summer, the sergeant called for Mr. Amblesby a little before ten o'clock. There had been a road accident the previous afternoon, and an inquest on the young motorcyclist who had died during the night in Flaxborough General Hospital was to be opened at eleven. An hour was not an overgenerous allowance for the collection of Mr. Amblesby, his rousing into awareness of what had happened and what he was supposed to do about it, and the arrangement of the old man in some semblance of official dignity at the coroner's table in Fen Street. He would also have to view the body in the hospital mortuary on the way.

Malley parked his car on the weed-dappled gravel outside Mr. Amblesby's front door. The hand-brake ratchet made a noise like a splintering plank. As the sergeant climbed out, the chassis rose four inches. It was an old car, nearly as big as a hearse but very tolerant.

The sergeant rang the bell and without waiting for an answer pushed open the front door and entered the dim, damp hall. He walked confidently over ten yards of bare, echoing tile and stood at the foot of a staircase. Peering up into the gloom, he called loudly but without urgency: "Are you there, sir?" It was a deep, amiable voice fattened upon oratorio.

In the upper distance, a door clicked. Slippered feet rustled to the stair head.

"Eh?" Sharp, querulous, hostile by habit.

"I've come to take you to the office, sir." In Malley's un-hurried hands was a tin of tobacco. He levered off the lid

9

and nudged the dark, aromatic flakes with his thumb. He looked at the tobacco carefully while he spoke. "There's another inquest for you to open. Eleven o'clock."

Mr. Amblesby was descending the stairs. He came slowly into what light filtered into the hall from the stained-glass panels in the front door. His black solicitor's clothes, half as old as himself and limp with wear, were too big for him. The jacket swung like a cloak.

The old man was holding something up to his face with both hands. Malley had the ridiculous fancy that it was a mouth organ. Then he saw that it was a kipper. The old man was nibbling at it with quick, determined little pecks.

"I thought you'd like a lift, sir," Malley said. "It's at eleven, the inquest. Just an opening."

"Eh?"

On reaching the foot of the staircase, Mr. Amblesby looked around for somewhere to put the kipper skeleton. It looked now like a comb. Malley took it from him and carried it to the front door, where he threw it into some shrubs.

Mr. Amblesby wiped his fingers on a big white handkerchief, which he then stuffed into his jacket pocket.

"You'll not want a topcoat," the sergeant told him.

Mr. Amblesby gazed sourly out past the door that Malley had left open. "Why not?"

"Because it's warm, sir. A lovely warm day. And you're coming in the car."

Malley always nursed the old man along with this half-comforting, half-chiding manner of a mental-hospital attendant. It was part of his revenge for the coroner's cruelty to others.

"That makes two," Malley remarked. "One still to come."

"Eh?"

"Inquests. We know that perfectly well, sir, don't we?

That inquests always come in threes. There'll be another before the end of the week."

He closed the door of the house behind them after dropping the latch. He hoped the old man had forgotten his key. He grasped his elbow and led him toward the rear door of the car.

Mr. Amblesby tugged away his arm. "Front. I like the front."

The sergeant shrugged. "Just as you like, sir. You know that seat's tilted, though, don't you? And slippery. You'll fall forward if you're not careful."

"It's the way you drive, Sergeant. If you drove properly, I'd not be thrown forward."

"All right, sir. I'll be very careful." He slammed the passenger door as if trying to stun a rogue elephant. The old man jumped and sat holding his ears.

"Sorry about that." Malley squeezed his bulk behind the wheel and drew his own door closed. It made no more noise than the click of a barrister's briefcase.

Mr. Amblesby crouched, staring straight ahead. After a while, he began raising his lower denture with his tongue and making it impinge against the thin, tightly drawn top lip. A faint rattling sound resulted, like pieces of broken porcelain jostled together in a bag.

Malley drove first to the hospital. He parked beside a low concrete building with a corrugated asbestos roof and four narrow windows covered with wire netting.

Inside, the coroner glanced indifferently at the face of the dead motorcyclist. The boy seemed very young, a child almost. A tousle of black hair was bunched high on the yellowish-gray, translucent flesh of the forehead. The hair, crisp and greasy, looked alive. But the face, unmarked except for the lightest of blue bruises over one cheekbone, was merely substance, inert and finished with.

11

The old man's wintry gaze passed on at once. He walked to the far end of the low, white-tiled room. Malley gently rearranged the sheet over the dead boy's face and followed the coroner.

Mr. Amblesby, suddenly interested now, clambered up on a platform. It was the balance on which corpses were weighed. A pointer swung a little part of the way around a big clocklike scale at the side of the machine. The scale was not visible to Mr. Amblesby. It was calibrated in kilograms. Malley looked at the pointer and took a diary from his pocket. He opened it at a folded back page of metric conversion tables.

Mr. Amblesby waited. "Well?"

The sergeant, frowning dubiously at the columns of figures, ignored him for another half minute.

The old man got off the platform and peered around the sergeant's arm. "Haven't you worked it out yet?"

Malley took some more time. At last he snapped the diary shut. "One hundred and fifteen pounds, sir. You've lost just over two pounds since last Thursday."

"Rubbish!" said Mr. Amblesby.

"Eight stone three," the sergeant repeated patiently. "Hundred and fifteen pounds. That's it." The diary went back into his pocket. "Sure you've not been overdoing things a bit, sir?" There was kindly anxiety on his pink face.

"Eh?" said the coroner.

Malley took the lead as they walked back to the mortuary door. There were four deep concrete steps to be climbed to ground level. On the top step, Malley switched off the light before opening the door. His large body kept the daylight off the steps behind him. He waited, listening. The old man's feet scraped uncertainly on the second step for a moment, but they gained the third safely. Malley felt a spiky finger impatiently jab his back. He turned.

"Mind you don't slip, sir." Malley held out a hand. The old man pushed past him and got in the car.

Twice on their journey to the police station the sergeant braked violently and without warning.

On the first occasion, he told Mr. Amblesby that a dog had run into their path. The coroner said that *he* had seen no dog. Malley's "You didn't, sir?" was sympathy itself.

The second emergency slid the coroner completely off his seat, hands flailing against the dashboard. He was unhurt but very angry. Malley invited him to share his own relief that a child's life had been spared. Mr. Amblesby stared at him as if at a madman.

"You mustn't worry, sir," Malley soothed. "We didn't even graze him."

Two witnesses were waiting in the small annex to the room on the first floor of the police headquarters where inquests were generally held. Mr. Amblesby paused on his way through and nodded to one of these people, a tall man with pure white hair carefully groomed back from a face tanned by holidays abroad. The man was seated as far apart as was possible in the ten-feet-by-six lobby from a dumpy, middle-aged woman in dark clothes. He gave a return nod but remained seated. The woman got up the moment Mr. Amblesby entered. Her chair tilted and knocked against the wall. She half turned and grasped it nervously, as if quieting a child in church.

In the farther room, under Mr. Amblesby's baleful eye, the doctor and the mother gave their evidence. To the doctor it was a familiar formality. His concise, velvet-voiced account of cranial fracture and laceration of the brain, consistent with the deceased's having been involved in a collision between two road vehicles, made the boy's death sound a proper and even laudable consummation. Mr. Amblesby, at any rate, was content. He delved noisily into a leather pouch and counted out the doctor's fee in silver. The doctor picked up the coins and slipped them into a watch pocket; he would be on the lookout, the action seemed to say, for blind beggars as soon as he reached the street. Then with a small bow to the coroner and a murmured "Good morning" to Malley, he glided from the court.

The mother's testimony—a matter of formal identification—was compressed into a single sentence. The body now lying at Flaxborough General Hospital had been viewed by her and was that of her son, Percy Thomas Hallam, age eighteen years, an assistant storekeeper, who resided with her at 5 George Street, Flaxborough.

And that, for the moment, should have been that. An adjournment for seven days. Malley waited for the old man to mutter his formula.

But Mr. Amblesby remained staring at the woman crossly. His mouth fell open a little in preparation for the dance of the dentures. Malley saw and was alarmed. He reached over to touch the woman's shoulder and said, "That's all for just now, Mrs. Hallam."

The dentures came forward and rose, then rattled back. "Have you been writing letters to me?" Mr. Amblesby asked.

Utterly confused, the woman looked at Malley and wonderingly shook her head.

"I'm asking you, not the sergeant," said the coroner.

Malley bent low to speak in Mr. Amblesby's ear. "There hasn't been any letter, sir. You mustn't question the lady like that."

The coroner flapped a dismissive hand. He did not take his eyes off Mrs. Hallam.

"I asked you whether you had written to me. You must know, woman."

"I haven't written to anybody, sir." The tips of gloved fingers moved back and forth, just touching her mouth. The glove was of black cotton and quite new.

"Eh?" said Mr. Amblesby.

Malley again intervened, his words loud and measured, as to someone deaf or feebleminded. "She says she hasn't written to anybody, sir. Not to anybody. There hasn't been a letter, sir."

Mr. Amblesby sat quite still, hunched in the center of the big, claw-footed chair. He went on looking at Mrs. Hallam. She began to weep quietly.

Suddenly the coroner flapped at her a dry, brown-mottled hand and thrust the other into the side pocket of his coat. He hauled out his handkerchief and draped it over his knees. A faint whiff of kipper reached Malley. After more groping, the old man held aloft a gray envelope. It had been slit open neatly in lawyer's style.

"Now tell me the truth. Did you send me this?"

"No, sir. I don't know anything about it."

Malley sighed, shaking his head. He firmly took the letter out of the old man's hand. He turned the envelope about, examining it, then withdrew and unfolded a sheet of gray notepaper. He stepped out of Mr. Amblesby's reach and began to read.

The coroner watched. He looked pleased, as though relishing the effect of a prepared surprise. The tip of his tongue, very wet and of the same color as a sheep's, curled over his upper lip.

Malley read the letter through twice. It was typed and unsigned. The type was of the slightly florid kind, italic characters matching up to form script, peculiar to certain portable machines.

15

Dear Friend: This is an urgent appeal. I am in great danger. The person whose loyal and faithful companion I have been—and to whom even now my life is dedicated—intends to have me done away with. I can scarcely believe his change of heart, but I have heard the plan discussed and must believe it, however unwillingly. They think I do not understand. Oh, how vain and ignorant! Of course I understand! I can sense when I am in the way. And I know that murder is going to be the reward for my uncomplaining loyalty. A poison pellet in my food . . . a quick injection . . . perhaps to be held helpless underwater by a loved hand until I drown . . . one or the other of these dreadful fates will overtake me if you, dear friend, do not bring aid. Soon I shall send you details of how you can help. I cannot—for reasons you will understand—sign this letter, but I enclose my photograph in the hope that your heart may be touched.

Malley turned the letter over, then looked inside the envelope. There was no photograph. He put letter and envelope on the table before the coroner.

"I think somebody's been pulling your leg, sir."

Mr. Amblesby's tongue disappeared; so did his look of triumph.

"Eh?"

"Whatever put it into your head"—Malley set about fussily tidying the papers, pen and inkwell in front of Mr. Amblesby—"that this had anything to do with Mrs. Hallam? You must try not to get things mixed up, sir." He turned. "Just sign your deposition, Mrs. Hallam. Then you can get along home."

The woman wrote her name with great concentration, as if frightened of spoiling something valuable but not her

16

own. Halfway through, she stopped and took off her glove. She wiped her hand on her black, thick coat, then completed the signature.

The sergeant took her to the door. Outside he spoke to her for some moments. She was silent and quite without curiosity. Malley told her to go home and make herself a cup of tea. He knew she probably would not have thought of it herself.

Malley found Mr. Amblesby peevishly pulling the knob of a cupboard.

"Where did you put my coat, Sergeant?"

"You haven't brought a coat, sir. You said you didn't need one."

"But it's raining."

Malley looked out of the window. It was indeed raining—heavily. He collected the two depositions from the table and slid them into a folder file. The page of typewritten gray notepaper was still there. He quickly glanced through it once more.

"Queer sort of letter, sir. When did you get it?"

"Eh?"

Malley resorted to booming pidgin. "This LETTER. Queer. When—did—you—GET—it?"

The old man gave the cupboard door a final shake. "Why don't you help me find my coat? It's raining."

Malley picked up the letter and put it in his pocket.

"Come along, sir. I'll take you back in the car."

2

MR. HARCOURT CHUBB, chief constable of Flaxborough, made it a rule never to open his mail until at least three hours after it had been delivered. It was not that he was a lazy or an inefficient man. Nor was he a coward. But experience had taught him that problems which were altogether raw and unpalatable at eight o'clock could acquire a manageable blandness by eleven. Some, indeed, seemed actually to evaporate through their envelopes if left undisturbed for a while. Thus he might ring the station around about noon and say: "Now then, what's all this about a Peeping Tom in Partney Gardens?" And somebody would get busy and eventually telephone back: "There's a Partney Drive and a Partney Avenue but no Partney Gardens, sir." Trouble disposed of. It happened time and time again.

It was with hope of his luck holding in this respect that Mr. Chubb telephoned Detective Inspector Purbright while he held before him a typewritten communication on gray notepaper. The time was a quarter to twelve.

"Ah, Mr. Purbright, nice to see the rain's eased off. Now then, what's all this about some woman expecting to be poisoned or drowned or something?"

There was a short silence.

"I'm afraid I'm not quite with you, sir."

"Oh, aren't you?" Mr. Chubb sounded surprised. "Well, I've had this letter, you see. I thought you might know something about it."

"No, sir."

"You don't?"

"No."

"I see. Yes. Well, it might just be a bit of silliness, you know."

Mr. Chubb waited, hoping the inspector would tell him there and then to throw the thing away, but all he got was a patient "Yes, sir?"

The chief constable frowned. He put the letter down and shifted the receiver to his other ear. "Perhaps I'd better read it to you. It's not signed, you know, and I can't think offhand of anyone who normally addresses me as 'Dear Friend.' Never mind, though. It goes on: 'This is an urgent appeal. . . .'"

Purbright listened dutifully. Mr. Chubb's reading style was that of a university professor transcribing the notes of a rival savant. He gave the impression of peering at an almost illegible scrawl and doing his best to render it into English prose.

When he had finished, Mr. Chubb waited again for the inspector's comment.

"I gather you don't take this letter seriously," Purbright said.

"Why do you think that?"

"Ah, you *do* take it seriously, then?"

"Everything must be judged on its merits, Mr. Purbright. I mean, here is a letter—unsigned—addressed to me by somebody or other who thinks they're going to be murdered. Or says they do . . ." He paused, sensible of

19

having strayed into dubious grammatical bypaths. "Anyway, I suppose you'll want to see it for yourself."

"That, if I may say so, is up to you, sir. The mode of address does sound rather personal."

"I don't think you need worry on that score, Inspector. The letter's here if you want to send a man around for it."

And with that, Mr. Chubb hung up. He felt, not for the first time, that his detective inspector might show more ready appreciation of his responsibilities.

Half an hour later, Constable Pooke arrived by bicycle at the chief's home.

He went to the side door by way of a gate bearing a white enameled plate with the words "No Peddlers." Pooke knew he was not a peddler, and the thought that he could pass where a whole profession, however humble and even noxious, was barred made the now sunny noontide all the more pleasing. He glanced approvingly at the forsythia and flowering currant that screened the front of the square, red-brick villa and admired the authentic striped effect that meticulous mowing had imparted to the small lawn. There was another lawn at the back, bordered by rose beds and a number of rigidly disciplined fruit trees. Between two of these, Pooke glimpsed the tall, silver-haired figure of Mr. Chubb. He was walking slowly in traversing movements over the grass and held before him what appeared to be a mine detector. As Pooke approached, he saw that the instrument was actually a long wooden stave with a shovel angled to its end. The chief constable, a breeder of Yorkshire terriers on a scale that even his fellow fanciers considered to verge on the immoral, was engaged in his daily Operation Clean Sweep.

As Pooke waited respectfully for Mr. Chubb to complete the last three traverses, he wondered where so many dogs could be corralled off. Their barking could be heard at some indeterminable distance. Within the house? Pooke —no peddler, he—paled at the thought.

However, the chief constable did not invite him in. He led him instead to a greenhouse, where he retrieved the letter from its place of safety beneath a potted cactus and handed it to Pooke.

"Inspector Purbright asked if you would like a receipt, sir. In view of the letter being your personal property, sir."

"That will not be necessary," Mr. Chubb said coldly. "My compliments to Mr. Purbright, and will you tell him that I have decided the letter was misdirected? He must do with it as he thinks best."

His gray gaze slid gently past the constable and settled upon a geranium, an errant shoot of which he reached across to pinch off. Pooke, feeling himself not merely dismissed but rendered nonexistent, said, "Sir", all by itself and departed.

It was not until midafternoon that a third letter, identical with those that had reached Mr. Amblesby and Mr. Chubb, arrived in the hands of its addressee, the editor of the Flaxborough *Citizen.*

George Lintz had been called the previous day to a conference at the London office of the group of newspapers that had bought the *Citizen* two years before. After sitting silently through the dismal and unintelligible wrangle that the chairman described, with considerable nerve, as "an inspirational get-together," he had missed the last train back to Flaxborough. He had slept badly in an expensive and hostile hotel. Worst of all, his thoughtless use of the out-of-date half of his cheap-rate return ticket had been triumphantly spotted by the clerk at Flaxborough Station, a man who remembered well the vain plea he once had made to Lintz for the keeping of his shoplifting mother-in-law's name out of the paper.

Not unreasonably, Lintz was in a somewhat sour mood by the time he began to explore the pile of such news copy and correspondence as his editorial staff had felt unable to deal with on its own.

Having reached, read and pondered the "Dear Friend" letter, he went to the door and summoned from an airless cubbyhole across the landing his chief reporter.

"What on earth is this bloody thing supposed to be about?"

Prile, the chief reporter, a narrow-faced, regretful-looking man with a probing fingertip permanently in one ear, offered no suggestion.

"What have you done with the photograph?" Lintz made a show of shuffling the papers on his desk top.

"There wasn't one."

"But it says here that whoever it is has enclosed a photograph. It's clear enough. And look, there's been something pinned to this corner." Lintz held the letter aloft for two or three seconds, then tossed it down. "God, I don't know. . . . I've only to be out of the office five minutes, and people start losing everything. Go and see if it's gotten into the reporters' room."

"That's all there was in the envelope. I opened it myself. Nothing but that. Definitely."

Lintz leaned back, tilting his chair almost to the wall. "Well, it's not very helpful, then, is it?"

"Definitely not." The chief reporter now was looking not only sad but bored.

Lintz brought his chair level again with a bang. "Make a copy straightaway. Then let me have that back. Don't write anything yet. If it isn't one of those bloody hoaxes, we ought to get a decent little story out of it."

"Oh, aye. Definitely." The chief reporter could as well have been acknowledging the likelihood of string vests being splendid protection against death by lightning.

He returned with a copy forty minutes later.

Lintz put it into the top drawer of his desk and pocketed the original. He locked the desk while the chief reporter was still looking. Then he took his hat from a derelict gas bracket beside the door and went out.

The chief reporter listened to Lintz clatter briskly down the stairs. He again crossed the landing to his own cell, and having wedged its broken chair into an angle of the wall, he sat in it and went immediately to sleep.

It was four o'clock, that pleasant downward slope of the Flaxborough day from which the prospect of an end to work, one hour distant, was clear and comforting. Lintz emerged from the *Citizen* Building into a street almost devoid of traffic. A couple of cars driven by women on their way to collect children from school went slowly past him and turned off onto Park Street. An old man wearing a thick blue fisherman's jersey sat on the curb, looking as if he might decide at any moment to set about replacing the slipped chain of his bicycle. From the doorway of a grocery store stepped a baldheaded man in a white coat. He gazed up and down the street, spotted Lintz, and briefly raised his hand. Then he concentrated all his attention upon an empty wooden box that lay at one side of his doorway. After a long while he moved it with his foot three inches farther north and stepped back to review it again. He was still thoughtfully regarding the box when Lintz turned the corner into Fen Street.

The police station was thirty yards along, on the left-hand side. It belonged to the same period as the municipal buildings and the town's washhouse (the latter recently demolished as a gesture of the council's good faith in private, as distinct from public, hygiene). The style was Edwardian Gothic, the material that peculiarly durable stone which looks like petrified diarrhea.

Lintz sought the entrance, which was halfway down a narrow passage at the side of the building. The small, rather sneaky doorway led to a dim corridor flagged with stone. On the right was a sliding window a foot square beneath a painted "INQUIRIES" sign.

Lintz went straight past the window and to the end of the corridor, where he pushed open a green-painted door and entered a bare hall, also with a stone floor. The hall seemed to serve no purpose other than to collect a mixture of noise from adjoining compartments. He heard the click of billiard balls, the rattle of thick china, the echo of a steel door being slammed, and what seemed to be the distant but lively banter of a team of big men in a small bathroom.

There was an iron spiral staircase in the opposite corner. It sagged and clanked beneath Lintz's weight as he climbed to the upper floor.

He found Inspector Purbright alone in an office furnished with a desk, a tall, chocolate-colored filing cabinet, two fairly capacious chairs, and a piece of carpet big enough to underlie not only the desk but one of the chairs as well, if it were drawn close.

Purbright was not sitting close to the desk. He was too tall, too long-legged to arrange himself otherwise than alongside it. As Lintz looked inquiringly around the door, the inspector turned to view him over his left shoulder.

"Mr. Lintz—how nice." He sounded genuinely pleased. A pen was forthwith capped and laid carefully beside some papers on the desk blotter. In Purbright's other hand appeared an open cigarette packet. He leaned sideways across the desk, offering it.

"Now, then," said Lintz, put just a fraction off balance

by the promptness of the inspector's courtesy. He lit a match as slickly as he could manage. "How's things?"

Purbright said they were so-so and conveyed by the rise of his eyebrows that the light extended by Lintz was the very thing he had been eagerly awaiting all afternoon.

These formal preliminaries observed, Flaxborough fashion, Lintz hastened to the substance of his call.

"We got a rather queer letter this morning. . . ." He reached into his pocket.

"Did you, now?"

"It may be all balls, but I thought you'd better take a look."

Purbright accepted the letter, unfolded it and read it through slowly. He put it down on the desk and continued to regard it while he stroked the back of his neck.

"I suppose," he said at last, "that you get a certain amount of fairly screwy correspondence." He saw Lintz start, as if offended, and said hurriedly: "What I mean is that I'd always understood that newspaper offices tend to attract the attention of cranks."

"Yes, but they usually sign their names."

"Oh, do they? So you think this one is uncharacteristic?"

"It's something new to me. I shouldn't have brought it in otherwise."

"No, you did quite rightly, Mr. Lintz. The trouble is that it doesn't really tell us anything, does it?"

"Not really. But can't these things be traced? I mean, I don't think that's meant as a joke. Whoever it is sounds— you know—serious, scared."

Purbright suppressed the faint smile brought by his glimpse of Lintz's ulterior professionalism. *Mystery letter sets police puzzle*. He shook his head.

"Virtually impossible in the ordinary way," he said. "On the face of it, this is just a bit of vague persecution mania.

There's been no crime reported with which we could connect it."

Lintz frowned. The affair was much less promising than he had allowed himself to hope.

"We'll hang onto it," Purbright said. "Make what inquiries we can. You never know."

Lintz shrugged and quickly stood up, running the brim of his hat between finger and thumb until the hat was in the right position to be lifted and put on in one confident movement when he turned toward the door.

"You'll let me know if—"

"If we turn anything up?" Purbright also was on his feet; he looked genially grateful. "Of course I shall."

Lintz nodded and turned. Up swept his hat as he stepped to the door.

"Oh, just one little point—"

Lintz looked back. He saw Purbright with the letter again in his hand.

"Photograph," Purbright said. "You didn't happen to see a photograph with this, did you?"

"There wasn't one. I asked Prile about that. He'd opened it, actually. He was quite definite."

"All right, Mr. Lintz. Many thanks."

3

"DO you happen to know," Inspector Purbright asked Detective Sergeant Sidney Love, "of anyone in this town who goes in fear of assassination?"

Love's pink, choirboy countenance set in thought. He seemed to find the question perfectly reasonable. Purbright watched him close, one by one, the fingers and thumb of his right hand, then, more hesitantly, three fingers of his left.

"Somebody's been writing around," Purbright said. He indicated the small collection on the desk. "One to old Amblesby, one to the paper, and one to the chief constable."

Love picked up the sheets, read one slowly and examined the others.

"They're all the same."

"Quite."

"Sort of circular."

"Sort of." Purbright knew better than to hustle his sergeant. Love's mental processes were more like plant growth than chemical reaction. They flowered in their own good time.

"Well written," Love observed after further consideration.

"That shortens your list, does it?" Purbright was recalling the silently fingered catalog of eight.

"Does away with it altogether. None of them could have put this together. Not on their own."

"The paper's a bit out of the ordinary."

"Classy," Love agreed, fingering it.

"You could try Dawson's and see if they stock it and if they remember who's bought any."

Love nodded. He was rereading parts of the letter to himself. Over certain phrases his eye lingered while his lips silently formed the words, savoring them. Purbright waited.

"I reckon a woman wrote it," Love announced at last. He looked suddenly pleased with himself.

"Do you think so?" Purbright's raised brows hinted without irony that he was ready to learn and to command.

"Well, look. . . ." Eagerness brightened the sergeant's face by several candlepower. "I mean, things like *loyal and faithful companion*—see?—and *loved hand*. And here—*heart may be touched*. Well, I mean, it must be a woman, mustn't it?"

"I suppose the phraseology is on the romantic side."

"It's downright sloshy."

"You may be right, Sid."

Nourished by this praise, Love took another, deeper plunge into deductive reasoning.

"This woman—there's more than just one trying to do her in. Here, you see—*They think I do not understand*—that's what she says. *They*. So there must be two of them."

"At least."

"Aye, well . . . Oh, I don't know, though—two's the usual, surely?"

There was a pause. Purbright felt a little mean at having disrupted the sergeant's happy theorizing.

"There's one thing I can't understand at all," he said

28

magnanimously. "Why does she say she can't sign the letter? Presumably she would have been immediately identifiable from the photograph that was supposed to be enclosed."

Love confessed that this point was very queer indeed, as was the absence of the photograph.

"She might have forgotten to put it into one of the letters, but it didn't come with any of them. And look here." Purbright pointed to the corner of each page. "There are pin marks on all three."

"She must have changed her mind," said Love.

"Possibly."

"Unless . . ."

Purbright looked at him with polite expectancy.

"Unless," said the sergeant, "somebody tampered with her mail."

"Ah," Purbright said. He put the letters aside with the air of having received a judgment upon them that would not soon or lightly be upset.

There were more pressing problems to be solved, certainly, than what had seemed from the outset to be an isolated spurt of crazy correspondence from some local victim of persecution mania.

As soon as Love had departed to make his inquiries at the shop of Mr. Oliver Dawson, bookseller and stationer, the inspector sent to the canteen for a mug of tea and turned his thoughts to charity.

Or more precisely, to charities.

Of these there were in Flaxborough forty-three known species. A further dozen undocumented examples were thought to exist, but evidence of their survival was unreliable. The biggest group—eighteen—was classifiable as canine. It included the O.D.C. (Our Dumb Companions), the Barkers' League, the Dogs at Sea Society, the Canine

29

Law Alliance and the Four Foot Haven. There were seven societies devoted specifically to the welfare of other domestic animals. A further six were dedicated to the protection of wild ones. Of the remaining twelve organizations, four could be said to have cornered the ministry of comforts to the human aged and three to have swept the board of orphans. The objects of the rest were of astonishing diversity and ranged from the reclamation of fallen gentlewomen to the Christianization of Mongolia.

It might be thought that the common motive of benevolence would have insured the mutual neutrality if not the cooperation of all these bodies. Inspector Purbright suffered no such delusion. He knew from long experience that the world of organized charity was one of contested frontiers, of entrenchments and forays. As far back as he could remember, the arrangement of a flag day or the timing of a fete had been as bitterly disputed as any filched military advantage. Membership of the various committees—a much-sought-after social cachet—had always carried the risk of assault, moral if not physical, by the unsuccessful contenders. Plots and counterplots went on all the time. The town council, practically every member of which had his or her own charitable ax to grind, was bullied this way and that on behalf of all causes in turn. Letters winged every other week into the columns of the Flaxborough *Citizen* bearing insinuations as nearly libelous as their authors (advised quite often by the editor, Mr. Lintz, who well knew the circulatory stimulus of correspondence just on the safe side of scurrility) dared render them.

Viewed dispassionately—or uncharitably, perhaps one should say—it was a lively sport that diverted into relatively harmless channels energy that might otherwise have fueled crime and commotion. As a policeman, a professional upholder of the queen's peace, Inspector Purbright

30

could not but approve. It was his earnest opinion, for instance, that had Alderman Mrs. Thompson lacked the vocation of preserving the lives of pigeons that roosted behind the balustrade of the public library, she would long since have done in Mr. Thompson and possibly a fair sprinkling of their neighbors as well. There were others he could call to mind whose equally unthinkable propensities had been sublimated into what the Flaxborough *Citizen* liked to term "tireless devotion to the well-being of the old folk of the town."

The public took it all in pretty good part. It was true that there had been casualties. These had mounted steadily with the increase in the number of street collections (practically every Saturday of the year was now a flag day in some cause or other). But not one victim cared to acknowledge that the reason for his injury had been an unseemly dash into traffic to avoid the solicitations of yet another flag seller. For the most part, the citizens of Flaxborough responded to calls on their charity with no less enthusiasm—and no more—than that with which they would have paid a bridge toll. Indeed, many of them vaguely supposed these demands to be ordained by authority—not the government, perhaps, but some kind of important consortium (of bishops, was it?) that also ran religion and cemeteries and Armistice Day and vaccination.

No, it was probably the recipients of the charity, or of what was left after expenses, for whom one really ought to feel sympathy, Purbright reflected. All those saved dogs, helpless in their havens, being patted by Mrs. Henrietta Palgrove. The poor old horses in the Mill Lane meadow, too decrepit and narrowly penned to escape their weekly "cheering up" by a mass muster of the Flaxborough Equine Rescue Brigade (or FERB). The orphans up at Old Hall

31

. . . Well, no perhaps not the orphans, he decided. They were well able to stand up for themselves, even against such an inveterate curl rumpler as Alderman Steven Winge, who had been bitten four times since Christmas. Purbright felt sorriest of all for the pensioners, the defenseless old men and women who week after week were jollied out of their peaceful cottages and trundled away to "treats"— usually at places like Brockleston-on-Sea, where they sat on hard benches at long board tables, there to be personally plied with tiny cakes and screamed solicitudes by ladies whom none had ever seen without hats and by gentlemen who looked as if they had smiled steadily, remorselessly, awake and asleep, since birth. . . .

Purbright gave a little shake of the head and resolutely hitched his chair nearer the desk. He opened a file marked "Charities; Incidents and Complaints" and began to read, not for the first time, the letters and reports it contained.

There was no doubt about it; Flaxborough's charity war had heated up alarmingly of late. Hostilities were beginning to bear the marks of professional generalship.

"Flower, sir? Buy a flower. Help the animals, sir."

Mr. Mortimer Hive found his progress along the narrow pavement of Market Street barred by a girl of fourteen or fifteen with big, earnest brown eyes and a mouth like pale pink candy. Slung from her neck was a tray of paper emblems. Mr. Hive glimpsed words along the front of the tray—KINDLY KENNEL KLAN—before a large slotted can, resoundingly cash-laden, was thrust to the level of his chin.

It was a highly inconvenient encounter for Mr. Hive, engaged as he was in following a woman whose native familiarity with Flaxborough streets put him, a London private detective, at disadvantage enough without the intervention of third parties.

However, good breeding made his response automatically chivalrous. He swept off his gray felt hat with one hand and thrust the other into the hip pocket of trousers whose cut, expensive and *de rigueur* in days when dinner and adultery were dressed for with equal fastidiousness, now looked oddly voluminous, like split skirts.

Mr. Hive selected a half crown from the withdrawn handful of change. The girl smiled happily at it and made a pick from the emblems on her tray. A plump little forearm nestled for a moment upon the lapel, old-fashionedly broad, of Mr. Hive's jacket. He felt a glow of pleasure, an almost fatherly benignity. He allowed a palmed penny to clink into the collection can and surreptitiously returned the half crown in his pocket.

"Delighted to be of assistance, my dear!"

The girl popped prettily back into the doorway from which she had accosted him, and with a final flourish of his hat, Mr. Hive was on his way.

The woman he had been following was now out of sight. He made what haste he could, consistent with courtesy, and sidestepped from time to time into the roadway to gain an extra yard or two whenever there was a gap in the traffic. This was a fairly perilous maneuver because the pedestrians were stubbornly disinclined to break ranks in order to let him rejoin them; it was rather like trying to haul oneself over the gunwales of an overcrowded lifeboat.

At last, anxious, out of breath and smarting from having been grazed by the tailboard of a truck, Mr. Hive spotted again the patch of bright lime green that was his quarry's hat. It was bobbing along in a tide of heads twenty yards away on the opposite side of the road.

Mr. Hive pressed forward but made no attempt to cross the road. By keeping close to the curb, he was able not only to maintain progress but to preserve an almost uninter-

rupted diagonal view of the respondent (no, no—the subject—he'd really have to master this new terminology).
And by the time she disappeared through a doorway, he
had no difficulty in seeing that she had entered the Market
Street branch of Flaxborough Public Library.

A minute later Mr. Hive also was in the building. He
mounted a short flight of stairs, pushed open a glass door
and found himself by a counter. Behind it, perched in a
sort of dock, a straight-haired young woman was ready
with a quick-freeze stare.

Mr. Hive affected not to notice.

There was a hiss. It sounded like "Tickets?"

He thought he was being asked to produce a ticket or
pass or something.

The young woman raised no further objection, but as
he walked on into the room, he had the impression that his
arrival had given her a shock of some kind. Covertly he
glanced down at his trousers. No, nothing amiss there.
Anyway, it had been something higher up that disturbed
her, he thought. Odd . . .

There were some dozen people at the shelves, all draped
in the attitude of slightly awed self-consciousness characteristic of book borrowers. Silence was almost absolute,
and several glances of censure were earned by the sucking
noises of satisfaction that emanated from an old man in the
biology section who had come in for a warm at Havelock
Ellis.

Mr. Hive made a quick survey. The subject was not in
the room. Then he noticed a second glass door. It was
marked REFERENCE. He walked nearer and peered through.

The woman in the green hat was bent, half kneeling, to
a shelf close to the floor in which a number of slender but
oversize volumes were stacked. She seemed to be replacing
one. Mr. Hive noted that its binding was pale blue and

34

tooled in gold. He thought it lay about eighth from the end of the row.

The woman got up and straightened her dress. As he had done several times before during the past three days, Mr. Hive took stock of her figure. It was plump but certainly not fat, with a lively curvaceousness which, though modified by strictly fashionable clothing, made a direct appeal to Mr. Hive's sense of beauty. He much regretted that his calling imposed so tenuous a relationship between him and his subjects. It was a mean, unnatural way of earning a living. How he longed sometimes to break cover, sweep up to the subject and grasp her hand, crying: Madame, I am Hive the detective at your service! Take supper with me, and you shall have my secrets!

She was reaching for the door. He stepped quickly aside and masked himself with a book. She walked past, behind him, with short purposeful steps. As he heard her turn by the counter and pause, her wake of perfume eddied around him. That, too, he liked about her. Lots of scent—very feminine. Most of them scarcely smelled at all nowadays.

In the empty reference room, Mr. Hive stooped and pulled out the book in the pale blue cover. It was one of a selection of operatic scores, *The Bartered Bride.* An appreciative smile lifted the corners of Mr. Hive's Menjouesque mustache. He riffled speedily through the pages of the score.

The scrap of paper was nearly at the end. He read its message without removing it, then closed and replaced the book. The whole operation had taken only twenty or thirty seconds. Mr. Hive felt distinctly encouraged; this was one of his better days.

A middle-aged woman with a little girl stood outside the door. Mr. Hive pulled it back and stood aside with a flourish to let them pass.

The woman thanked him mournfully and began to advance into the reference room, ushering the child before her. Then quite suddenly she stopped and stared, first unbelievingly, then with disgust and horror, at Mr. Hive.

Painfully disconcerted as he was, Mr. Hive recognized in the silent convolutions of the woman's mouth an opportunity for lipreading practice. It gave him no trouble at all.

Filthy beast . . .

Clutching the child to her skirts, she gazed angrily about her as if in search of some strong-armed champion. Mr. Hive saw that his wisest course was prompt disengagement. He strode toward the exit.

As he approached the counter, he noticed that the librarian who had hissed at him was now in anxious conference with a tall, angular, bald-headed man, doubtless a senior colleague well versed in the handling of filthy beasts.

Both looked up together. The man made a movement suggestive of challenge.

Mr. Hive avoided looking at him and marched straight for the door. It would not have surprised him in the least to hear the clanging of an alarm bell and the rushing descent of steel shutters. But nothing happened, and he was soon safely immersed in the throng of Market Street.

Was there any point in again picking up the trail of the subject? He thought not. The message she had implanted in the third act of *The Bartered Bride* was specific as to the time and place of her assignation.

Anyway, he wanted to get back as soon as possible to the privacy of his lodgings. The long bedroom mirror seemed to hold the best hope of his being able to solve the mystery of the outraged women in the library.

Had he unknowingly collected some horrid stigmata? A mark of plague? Delicately Mr. Hive ran fingertips over his cheeks. An intimation of evening stubble, nothing more. He thrust from his mind a certain ridiculous but disturbing suspicion dating from his boyhood reading of *The Picture of Dorian Gray*.

Mr. Hive eased the slim gold pocket watch from its fob and pressed the catch. The outer case sprang open to reveal the twin bits of information that the time was a quarter to five and that the watch had been presented "To Mortimer Hive, In Appreciation—Roly" over the arms of the Marquess of Grantham. It was the arms of the marchioness, a muscular and predatory lady from Wisconsin, that Mr. Hive had cause chiefly to remember ("It was like a night in the python house," he had averred afterward to the Granthams' family solicitor), but he bore old Roly no ill will and still treasured the watch that had accompanied his fee.

A quarter to five was an ideal time, he reflected, to send in his report. He entered the next telephone booth he came to and dialed a local number.

"Dover?" inquired Mr. Hive guardedly.

"That's right."

"Hastings here. All right if I—"

"Yes."

"I commenced observation of Calais at ten twenty hours, when she left the house accompanied by a large dog. She went to a park near the river, apparently in order to let the dog have some exercise, which it did."

"Liver and white markings?"

"I beg your pardon?"

"The dog. Liver and white."

"Ah . . . yes." Mr. Hive did not really remember.

"Fine animal, didn't you think?"

"Most captivating."

"All right. Carry on."

"Calais remained in the park until"— Mr. Hive consulted an envelope—"until eleven thirty hours. It was raining heavily for part of the time, and—"

"She didn't let the dog get wet, did she?"

"No, no, she took it into a shelter and sat there until the rain stopped. I was able to observe that no one made contact with the subject while she was in the park. Afterward she went into several shops and returned home at twelve fifteen hours, when I took the opportunity of going back briefly to my lodg—my hotel and changing into dry clothes."

Mr. Hive paused and made ready to wave aside his client's expressions of sympathy, but none were offered.

He went on. "At fifteen hundred hours, Calais came out of the house and continued on foot into town. She entered a tea shop called the Willow Plate and was joined almost immediately by a woman whom I suggest we code-name Dieppe."

"What did she look like?"

"Billiard-table legs, poor soul. But a vivacious manner. Spectacles of a somewhat bizarre, transatlantic cast. Light, fluffy hair. Loud voice. Thirty-five or so."

"I think I know who it was."

"A vodka-and-lime sort of woman. A virgin, for a ducat." Mr. Hive stretched elegantly against the side of the booth and flicked the glass with his yellow wash-leather gloves. He smiled gently into space, as if recalling some charming childhood fiction.

"No need to be offensive."

"Offensive?" Mr. Hive's bewilderment was genuine.

"Never mind. Go on. Did you hear what they were talking about?"

"Some of it, certainly. I succeeded in finding a seat in the next alcove thing to theirs—it is that kind of tea shop, you know—and I was able to take notes of parts of the conversation until nearly sixteen hundred hours, when they left separately. Calais was very difficult to hear. Dieppe was not. I received what you might call the drift. Shall I summarize it for you?"

"I simply want to know what arrangement they made. I take it that an arrangement *was* made."

"Yes, indeed," declared Mr. Hive, peering again at his envelope and turning it the other way up. "Briefly, it is this: Dieppe is to travel tonight to Nottingham—"

"What is Nottingham the code for?"

"Nothing. Nottingham is just Nottingham."

"So long as we know."

"She is going there tonight by train. She will book a single room at the Trent Towers Hotel, but in Calais' name, not her own. She will not leave again until tomorrow morning, when she will check out, do some shopping and catch the eleven o'clock train back to Flaxborough. At Flaxborough Station, Dieppe will be met by Calais, to whom she will give the things she has bought, together with her hotel receipt."

There was a pause.

"You have done rather well, Mr., ah, Hastings."

"All part of the job, Mr. Dover." Mr. Hive beamed through the glass at an anxious-looking young woman who had been standing outside the booth for the past five minutes. He raised his gloves and pursed his lips in a way that intimated his imminent abandonment of the telephone. Instead of looking grateful, however, she gave a scowl of disgust (at his chest, he thought) and hastened away, muttering.

Mr. Hive, feeling more conscious than ever of having mysteriously and innocently become the object of public odium, delivered the rest of his report.

39

"Good man," said Dover. "That message she left, though . . ."

"For Folkestone, presumably," said Mr. Hive.

"Oh, for Folkestone without doubt. But will you repeat it? I want to get it absolutely right."

"It was: 'All fixed for tonight. Wait at cottage.' "

" 'Wait at cottage.' "

"Yes."

"And you know where the cottage is? At Hambourne Dyke? You remember my directions?"

"Clearly," said Mr. Hive.

4

"THERE'S a Miss Cadbury would like a word with you. She's the secretary of the"—Sergeant Love glanced down dubiously at the card in his hand—"of the Kindly Kennel Klan."

"She's not wearing a white hood, is she?" The day's worries had left Purbright with a tendency to be rather reckless in the matter of jokes.

"No," said Love. "I don't think it's anything to do with religion."

. Miss Cadbury, agitatedly fumbling at the amber beads around her neck, was already through the doorway.

"It's our flag day, Inspector. And some perfectly dreadful things have been happening."

Purbright soothed her into a chair. He motioned Love to close the door.

Miss Cadbury was a big, gaunt woman with a downy chin. The restlessness of her hands emphasized their largeness. She had knees to match. She wore a mauve woolen costume and a peaked felt hat that looked designed to deflect falling masonry.

"Now, then, Miss Cadbury, what are these dreadful things that have happened?"

For fully half a minute, she stared at him, tight-lipped. Purbright hoped that this was just for dramatic effect and did not presage some personal accusation.

"The committee," she said at last, "is extremely upset. What people are saying, I daren't imagine. I only hope that those responsible . . ."

Purbright waited, looking suitably grave. He saw that the woman's big, strong fingers were straying around the clasp of her handbag. The bag was a massive hide affair; its clasp looked as if it would require a set of keys.

Miss Cadbury squared her shoulders. "Let us not beat about the bush, Inspector. My organization's name has been brought into disrepute by a trick, a very nasty trick. Certain unauthorized persons have been passing themselves off as our flag sellers."

"Today, you mean?"

"Of course. I have lost no time in letting you know. You must do something about it."

"Perhaps you could be a little more specific, Miss Cadbury. Can you tell me where any of these people are operating?"

"No, I cannot."

"You haven't actually seen one yourself, then?"

"It has been going on. There is no doubt about that. I have been given . . . well, evidence."

"What kind of evidence?"

"Very upsetting evidence." Her fingers were firm now upon the handbag fastening. Purbright again marveled at the robustness of the clasp. What had she got in there—a pet eagle?

"A number of people have come into the flag-day head-

42

quarters," Miss Cadbury went on. "They have complained very bitterly. As well they might, although we ourselves, of course, were in no way to blame. We tried to convince them of that, but these things take an awful lot of undoing."

"It might be of some assistance," Purbright said, "if you were to tell me what they were complaining *about*. I mean, how did they know that they had made contributions to unauthorized collectors? I can appreciate that this worries *you*, but why should distinction between official and unofficial soliciting worry ordinary members of the public?"

"We do *not* solicit!" Miss Cadbury's august indignation proclaimed a bosom he would not have given her credit for.

Sergeant Love helpfully intervened. "It's some of the flags that have been the trouble, sir. I think they've given offense."

"Ah," said Purbright. "Perhaps you would tell us about that, Miss Cadbury."

She nodded. "Unauthorized emblems very like our own but quite, quite unauthorized have gotten into circulation. There are"—she hesitated—"words on them."

"Aren't there words on yours?"

"Not *these* words."

The inspector's obtuseness could not have been more eloquently reproved.

"They were, as you might say, messages," Miss Cadbury resumed after a while. "Printed very boldly upon a clever imitation of our emblem. Perhaps *message* is not quite the right description, though." She frowned.

"No?"

"No. Invitations. And of the most embarrassing kind."

Love again was ready to elucidate. "Like at fairs, sir. You know, on funny hats."

43

The huge handbag clicked and gaped dramatically. "There is nothing funny," boomed Miss Cadbury, "about *these,* Inspector!"

Down in the town, there was no longer the rattle of a single collecting can, authorized or unauthorized, to be heard. The workers for the Kindly Kennel Klan had abandoned their strategic pitches and converged upon the committee rooms on Catherine Street. While they sat and gratefully sipped tea around a field kitchen urn borrowed for the occasion from the Civil Defense people (*Note: in case of atomic attack, emergency urn at 41 Stanstead Gardens*), a fresh relay of Miss Cadbury's workers cascaded coins upon a long trestle table and counted the take.

Mr. Hive had returned with all possible speed to his lodgings after telephoning his report, and having spent five minutes in puzzled scrutiny of his reflection in the wardrobe mirror, had hit at last upon the cause of the horrified response of the ladies he had encountered in town. Removing the emblem from his buttonhole—its printed promise was terse and of the most extreme indelicacy—he had transferred it to the breast of a life-size engraving of the prince consort that hung over the mantelpiece, where it looked like a sort of jaunty Good Housekeeping seal of sexual prowess.

Now, thoughtfully sipping gin from a thick-walled tumbler, Hive surveyed the things set out upon the table. They were a ponderously old-fashioned half-plate camera, some plate holders, a box of flashbulbs and a battery. He tested the battery with a flash-lamp bulb mounted on callipers, then slipped it into a recess in the camera. He packed all the equipment into a battered hide carrying case with a long leather shoulder strap and set it down near the door. Finally, after consulting the Marquess of Grantham's appreciative watch, he refilled his tumbler and reclined with a sigh on the bed.

At Flaxborough Station, a train was coming in. It was the third and last train of the day for Nottingham. Among the twenty or so people on the platform were a man and a woman who had the constrained air of having just suspended an argument for the sake of public appearance. The woman, who wore a bright green hat and carried a small dressing case, was frowning and silent. Her companion, though equally taciturn while the train rumbled and squealed to a halt, wore an expression of kindly but determined concern. He pointed to an empty compartment and stepped before her to open the door. The woman spoke at last. "I told you there'd be plenty of room. There was no need at all for you to come."

She got into the carriage and perched, stiff with resentment, in the corner seat. The man remained on the platform. He was about to shut the door when he caught sight of a woman in the act of boarding the train a few yards away. He shouted and waved. The other woman looked very surprised. Again he waved. She hesitated for several seconds, then, forcing a smile, came toward him. He cheerfully ushered her into the compartment and slammed the door. The train began to move. The man on the platform watched until the last carriage glided out past the signal box and the level crossing gates swung back to release the pent stream of cars and bicycles at the station's west end. Then he turned and walked toward the exit. His smile of persevering solicitude had broadened into one of amusement.

The streets were full of bicycles, clattering droves of them, bowling homeward from the docks and timber yards and factories. The riders sensed that by sheer weight of numbers they had taken over the town just for that hour.

45

Timber men, packers, engineers, men from the wharves converged in speeding groups which then split at junctions and crossroads with banter and shouts of farewell. The older men, riding alone or in pairs, let the others pass while they sat in straight-backed dignity on their saddles and showed off their skill at lighting pipes with one hand. They affected not to notice the antics of the boys who stood on their plunging pedals like rodeo performers or crouched, chin to handlebars, and furiously raced one another, with the squeals of the cannery girls as prizes.

The shops were closing. Not brusquely, as in a city, but with an accommodating casualness. Time in Flaxborough was, like most other things, a matter of compromise. Thus at twenty to six, Sergeant Malley was not in the least surprised to find unlocked the door of a butcher whose business was supposed nominally to cease at five o'clock. He went in and bought some pressed beef for his supper. In natural deference to the coroner's officer's calling (and perhaps the butcher's, for that matter) the small talk was of bodies.

"Two this week," the sergeant confirmed. "One natural, as it turned out. The other was young Perce Hallam."

"Oh, aye, the motorbike business."

"Trouble is, they always come in threes. Always. And now I feel I can't get on with anything. You know, like the bloke in the hotel bedroom waiting for that bugger upstairs to drop his other shoe."

"What bugger upstairs?"

"The one with three legs."

As the sergeant emerged from the butcher's shop, a blue town service bus went by on its way to Heston Lane end. In it, three seats from the driver on the left-hand side, sat a woman with a serene, going-home, face.

She was Mrs. Henrietta Palgrove, aged forty-three,

46

housewife, of Dunroamin, Brompton Gardens, Flaxborough, charity organizer, voluntary social worker, animal lover.

The bus drove slowly through the emptying town and stopped to pick up its last passengers at St. Lawrence's Church and Burton Place. Then it entered Burton Lane and began a rambling tour of two council estates. Ten minutes later, its load reduced and in the opinion of Mrs. Palgrove refined, it turned toward the complex of avenues south of Heston Lane, malevolently described by envious occupants of less substantial and secluded residences as "Debtors' Retreat."

Mrs. Palgrove alighted at the top nearest the upper end of Brompton Gardens and made her way home. Except for her, the road was empty. It usually was. The people who had settled here had done so expressly in order to avoid sight of one another. They were as apprehensive of being "overlooked" as their medieval ancestors had been of coming within scope of the evil eye. Only from an occasional flash of red tile or brick through high foliage could one have guessed that Brompton Gardens was populated at all.

Dunroamin was the last house but one on the left before the road narrowed abruptly to become a graveled track through open fields. This track eventually doubled back toward town and joined the main road into Flaxborough from Chalmsbury. The house was screened not only by the thick beech hedge more than ten feet high that bordered its surrounding gardens but by a pair of enormous old chestnut trees in the middle of the front lawn. A drive of new-looking concrete skirted the lawn and ran past the side of the house to open out into a broad paved area, a sort of courtyard, brightened by geraniums and azaleas growing in cast concrete urns. From the courtyard's opposite side, a path wide enough to give passage to a car led between rose beds and more lawns to a two-car garage. This was built of concrete blocks roughened to simulate stone and was half hidden by creeper. Just beside it, a gate in the beech hedge opened to a back lane.

As Mrs. Palgrove approached the house, she heard the murmur of a car engine. Suddenly the sound expanded to a roar. It died, rose again, died.

Frowning, she looked across to the end of the garden. More bursts of noise, like the protests of a teased and tethered beast. And with each, a little cloud of azure smoke came rolling out of the open garage.

Leonard Palgrove, aged forty-four, company director, chamber of commerce member, amorist *manque,* sports-car enthusiast, was making love to his Aston Martin.

Mrs. Palgrove smiled, but not fondly, and walked on. In the court of the concrete urns, she paused to set something down. It was a dog, but one so diminutive that it had been invisible in its carrying place between the crook of Mrs. Palgrove's arm and the overhang of her bosom. Released, it pranced like a high-stepping rat to the nearest urn and lifted against it a leg no bigger than a pigeon's drumstick. She spoke to the dog, calling it Rodney. She crooned it a number of questions. Rodney made no reply.

Leaving the door open, Mrs. Palgrove walked through the cool, gray-carpeted hallway and entered the kitchen. This was an impeccable, gleaming laboratory in saffron and white. Mrs. Palgrove set down upon the central table the square cardboard box that had hung by its looped ribbon from her finger all the way from Penny's Pantry. She untied the ribbon and carefully lifted the lid of the box. There rose the sugared, buttery smell, faintly tinged with violet and almond essences, of freshly made cakes. Mrs. Palgrove reached across to the window and pulled the cord

48

of the air-extraction fan. Then she lifted the cakes one by one from the box and arranged them on a plate fashioned to resemble a huge, glossy vine leaf. After regarding the collection for a few moments, she transferred a Chocolate Creme Log to a saucer, which she put down on the floor. "Rodney!" she cried.

At third calling, the dog appeared. It licked some of the icing off the cake, then wandered away, bored. Mrs. Palgrove stooped and cut the cake into small, neat cubes. The dog returned to sniff at them. "Cakey," declared Mrs. Palgrove. "Nice!" Despite her repeating both these observations several times and quite vehemently, Rodney did not respond. Mrs. Palgrove called him a naughty boy in the end and went off into the lounge on her own, carrying the rest of the cakes.

Her husband joined her ten minutes later, just in time for a solitary Coconut Kiss. He ate it quickly, standing up. Mrs. Palgrove watched with distaste the absentminded way he rubbed his stickied fingertips on one of the chintz chair covers. She picked up the empty plate and took it to the kitchen, where she washed and put it away.

"Got to go to Leicester tonight," Leonard announced as soon as she was in the room again. He was still standing; he believed that standing was a sound way to keep weight down.

Leicester. Seventy or eighty miles. So that's why he had been tinkering with that car of his. . . .

"Why should you want to go to Leicester?"

"I don't *want* to go. I said I *have* to. Business."

"You'll be late back, then?"

He turned, shrugging. "Lord, I'm not dragging back here the same night. I'll stay over. Perhaps Tony can put me up."

"Tony?" The tone implied that this was the first she had ever heard of a Tony, in Leicester or anywhere else.

"He's with Hardy-Livingstone. *You* know him. Drives an Alvis."

"You can't just drop in on people like that. They aren't hotelkeepers."

"Tony won't mind. His wife won't, either."

She looked at him bleakly. "What is it you're going to do in Leicester?"

"Something to do with—with machinery. It wouldn't mean anything to you."

"It means something to me that without any warning you clear off to stay the night with some people or other I've never heard of."

"But you *have* heard of him. Tony Wilcox. Bloody hell, you met him at the firm's dinner a year ago. Two years, maybe."

"Two years ago?"

"Yes."

"You went on your own two years ago. I was having that sinus operation."

"Well, three, then. What the hell does it matter?"

"Quite a lot, judging from the way you're taking refuge in obscenities. It's always the same when you've something to hide."

Palgrove's gaze went to the ceiling. "Oh, for Christ's sake . . ."

It was, on the face of it, a fairly standard quarrel. The neighbors would not have given it much of a rating even if they had heard it, which they hadn't. One fortuitous eavesdropper there was, however, whom the wrangle impressed. He was the boy from Dawson's, delivering the evening newspaper. This boy had been reared in the very proper belief that rows were the prerogative of ordinary folk and

50

had no place in the well-ordered lives of the sort of people who lived in Brompton Gardens. So when he heard coming through the slightly open window of Mrs. Palgrove's posh lounge some of the familiar expletives of home, he loitered in wonderment.

5

BY the time Mr. Hive judged that to descend from his room would no longer entail the risk of being way-laid by his landlady, aggressively hospitable and redolent of fish cakes, he had consumed three-quarters of a bottle of gin. He was now quite confident that even if Mrs. O'Brien had not yet cleared away such remnants of her daunting evening meal as she had been unable to coax and bully down the gullets of her other "gentlemen," he at least was proof against persuasion.

It so happened that his optimism was not put to the test. Mrs. O'Brien was off patrol, safely detained in her back kitchen by the gossip of a visiting neighbor.

Closing the street door as softly as he could behind him, Mr. Hive set down upon the step the huge camera case that he had hugged close, for fear of its bumping the banisters, during his tiptoe descent of the stairs. He touched his lilac silk cravat, stroked his mustache, and drew on one glove. He then slung the strap of the case over his left shoulder and walked as briskly as the load would allow to where he had parked, a few yards down the road, his small and elderly motorcar.

The car drew up five minutes later in the cobbled yard of the Three Crowns Hotel.

Mr. Hive's was the first arrival of the evening in the bar known as the Chandlers' Room, a name that survived from days when corn merchants in particular frequented it, passing around their little canvas bags of grain samples and swallowing Hollands and water from mugs as big as drench buckets. It was a low, paneled room that received little light from the narrow lane outside, but in recent years more lamps had been set in the ceiling while a rhubarb-pink glow emanated from the mirrored alcove behind a modern bar. The roof beams were genuine enough; their bowed and blackened oak gave the impression that the room was being gradually squashed by the rambling old house above and would one day admit only customers prepared to drink lying down.

Mr. Hive, who was as yet nowhere near that extreme, nevertheless had to incline his head once or twice as he crossed from the door to the bar.

There was no one behind the bar. Mr. Hive put his case down on the floor and rested one foot on it while he peered through a doorway into the farther room from which he supposed service would arrive.

A girl—appraised by Mr. Hive at once as a delicious girl, with ripe lips parted in helpful inquiry, plump white arms, and a positive reception committee of bosom—rose from a table where she had been writing in a ledger and came toward him.

Mr. Hive removed his hat and lightly kissed the fingertips of his right hand.

He had intended to stay on gin, but that, he saw, would not now be suitable.

"I wonder, my dear, if you would be good enough to let me have some brandy?"

"What, to take out?" The barmaid, quite unused to circuitous gallantry, supposed that Mr. Hive must be a doctor wanting a restorative for somebody who had collapsed on the street.

He smiled. "I am scarcely likely to wish to consume it away from premises graced by so charming a person as yourself!"

She worked this one out, then turned to reach down a bottle. "Single?"

"No; a double, I fancy, would be more appropriate." He gazed contentedly down her cleavage while she measured the drink.

She set the glass on a pink tissue mat and pushed nearer a jug of water and a soda siphon. "Seven shillings, please, sir."

Mr. Hive made a small, elegant bow of the head and drew a handful of change from his hip pocket. He held the coins in the extended palm of one hand and made unhurried selection from them. The operation served to display slim, clean and dexterous fingers, also faultlessly laundered cuffs whose gold links were in the semblance of crossed rowing sculls. These the girl observed and indicated. "Pretty," she said.

He looked at the links as if noticing them for the first time. He closed the hand with the money in it and turned it this way and that to make the little gold oars catch the light. "Relics of youthful athleticism," he said, musingly. Then, brightening: "Oh, I don't know. Henley, forty-eight—it's not all that long ago. I daresay I could still stroke an eight."

"I'll bet," the girl said.

Mr. Hive put both hands in his pockets and gazed into the middle distance. His expression of benign abstraction spoke of long, golden afternoons on sun-dappled water, of the rhythmic creak of oarlocks, of a bow wave's glug in the holes of river creatures. . . .

"Ah, well." He reached for the glass. "Here's very good health to you, dear lady!"

"Cheers," the girl murmured softly. She waited until he had taken two or three ruminative sips of the brandy. "All right?"

Mr. Hive half closed one eye and pouted. "Superb!" he declared.

The girl nodded. "Seven shillings then, please, sir."

With a fierce scowl of self-blame, Mr. Hive rapped his forehead several times, then reached anew for money. This time he counted it assiduously into her waiting hand.

Other customers began to come into the bar. Mr. Hive picked up his drink and his case and with a final glance of admiration at the twin moonrise of flesh over the barmaid's bodice took himself off to a table at the side of the room opposite the door.

Twice in the next twenty minutes he went back to the bar to renew his order and, he hoped, to gain further favor in the eyes of the splendid young woman behind it.

On his first reappearance she had asked, with becoming casualness: "Where are *you* from, then?" and he had invited her to guess, whereupon she had shaken her head coyly, and he had rewarded her with the quotation "From Dunbar's 'Flower of Cityes Alle.'" "Well I never," she'd replied. "You don't *look* Scotch."

Now he was before her again, presenting her with his empty glass as if it were a rose. She busied herself with the bottle and the little pewter measure. Mr. Hive glanced about him for an opening, nonliterary this time, to further conversation. He noticed a box on the counter, a little to the left of his elbow. It was a collecting box, and there was something about it, something oddly familiar, that caused him to pull a pair of spectacles from his breast pocket and read the label.

"Gracious me!" he exclaimed.

The girl looked up. She saw a grin of delighted recognition overspread her customer's face.

"Lucy . . ." Mr. Hive murmured to himself. He was looking happily abstracted again.

"Lucy who?"

"Mmm . . ."

"Never mind." The girl put the refilled glass on one of the little pink mats. Mr. Hive paid without being prompted.

"Tell me, my dear," he said with sudden resolution, "if you know who brought this box in here. It wasn't, by any chance, a lady from London? A well-spoken, ah, personable lady?"

"I don't know whether she came from London. She lives here now. In Flax."

"Does she? Does she, indeed?"

"That's right." The girl regarded the box indifferently. She seemed to be in no degree emotionally involved with the New World Pony Rescue Campaign. "I'm trying to remember her name. Funny sort of name . . ."

"Miss Lucilla Teatime," crisply announced Mr. Hive.

"Yes." The girl giggled. "That's it. Teatime!" Instinct told her to keep hilarity in check. "Friend of yours?" she asked.

"A very old friend—and an altogether admirable lady."

"She seemed very nice."

"I'm happy to think you have had the privilege of knowing her."

"Well, she doesn't come in all that often, actually," said the girl. "Just to see to the box, you know."

Mr. Hive nodded. "An indefatigable worker for good

causes." He again examined the box on the bar, this time a little narrowly; then he gave it an affectionate pat. "One of her favorite charities, that one," he declared.

He returned to his seat. There were now seven or eight other people in the room. He surveyed them one by one over the top of his glass and decided that he liked them all, from the young couple with bright country complexions and a careful way of sitting to the ruminating old farmer whose extraordinary facial resemblance to a sheep was emphasized by his habit of emitting at the end of each swig of his beer a quiet little "baaa."

Mr. Hive had just begun his fourth double brandy when three men entered the bar in a group. For a few moments they stood just inside the door while the foremost glanced searchingly around the company.

He was a man of medium height with thin, brushed-back hair of no particular color, a plump but sallow face and unblinking, protuberant eyes. His way of leaning forward from firmly planted feet suggested a readiness to be launched at very short notice. Even had Mr. Hive not known who this man was, his powers of deduction would have told him that here was the classic attitude of preparedness for boys' wicked wiles: the stance of a schoolmaster.

As it was, he recognized at once Mr. Kingsley Booker, M.A., fourth-year form master and teacher of geography, religion and swimming at Flaxborough Grammar School. Mr. Booker's two companions he did not know, but he felt sure he was going to like them. He donned a smile in readiness.

Brooker saw Hive and said: "Ah." He came across the room at a slightly increased angle of forward tilt, as if talking against a stiff wind. He made introductions.

"Mr. Mortimer Hive . . . Mr. Clay—my headmaster."

Mr. Hive shook the soft, very warm hand of a brisk and

57

tubby man who regarded him with eager concentration. Mr. Clay had the cleanest, shiniest face Mr. Hive had ever seen. His little beak-shaped nose was absolutely smooth, like pink porcelain, and had almost as high a polish as the lenses of the pince-nez it supported.

"And this is Mr. O'Toole, the county youth employment coordinator."

"Now then, cocky," said Mr. O'Toole affably. He did not offer his hand but turned at once to satisfy himself that some sort of drink-buying facilities existed in the room.

Hive asked what he could have the pleasure of fetching them. Mr. Clay said after some consideration that a small and extremely dry sherry would be very nice. Mr. Booker said he fancied to try this lager and lime that he had heard people talk about. Mr. O'Toole said: "Pint of wallop."

The girl behind the bar looked pleased to hear Mr. Hive's four-part order. "You've made some friends, then? That's nice." She set about the wettest part of the job first —pulling a pint of mild ale for the youth employment coordinator.

"Oh, it's a sociable little town," said Mr. Hive.

She poured a Tio Pepe, then a British-type lager which she vaccinated with a heavy dose of lime cordial. "For the ladies," she announced waggishly. Mr. Hive was about to correct this misconception but decided to let it stand and to take whatever credit it might reflect.

Mr. Booker helped to dispense the drinks around the table. The action revealed a big leather patch on each elbow of his tweed jacket. Both the jacket and the buttoned woolen cardigan beneath it looked as if they had been lived in for a considerable time.

Mr. Clay accepted his sherry with a prim little nod that was in character with his general economy of movement

58

(Must have a very tight skin, mused Mr. Hive. Poor fellow) and put it down some distance off, as though he intended to save it for Christmas.

"You are from London, I gather?" said the headmaster.

Mr. Hive acknowledged that he was.

"A city of great opportunity."

"Boundless."

"You will appreciate, Mr. Hive, that for our young people London is a magnet. To them it promises fulfillment. We educationists may have a more skeptical view— and with good cause, I venture to say—but we do not flatter ourselves that we can correct the naïve assumptions of youth. Only experience can do that."

Mr. Hive heard beside him a short, bitter laugh. It came from Mr. O'Toole, who was rubbing the side of his jaw with the rim of his already empty glass. This friction made a curious sound—describable perhaps as a rasping tinkle.

"What the headmaster is leading up to, I think—"

"Now, Booker, pray allow me to do my own leading. Mr. Hive will see it's object soon enough." Mr. Clay inclined a little closer to Mr. Hive and waited for him to make a quick swallow of what remained of his brandy. He continued. "We arrange from time to time at the school what we term a careers symposium. It is attended by boys of the fifth and sixth forms, and they are able to put questions to representatives of a variety of professions whom we invite as guests."

"What a splendid idea!" exclaimed Mr. Hive.

A tiny smile of pleasure augmented the glints and gleams of the headmaster's polished face. "We have, I think I may say, found the idea a useful one."

"Splendid!" (Mr. Hive had decided that "splendid" was a splendid word.)

"Quite. Now it so happens that just such a symposium

59

has been arranged for this evening, in, ah, twenty-five minutes' time. The panel—I fancy that is the word—is a not undistinguished one. We have been promised the attendance of a solicitor, also a real estate agent, an inspector of police, and a—let me see—a manager of a sawmill, I believe.

"Unfortunately—and I come now to the point I have had in mind ever since Booker here happened to mention your presence in the town, Mr. Hive—unfortunately, I say, all these gentlemen follow their professions locally. Sound men, you understand, very sound. But I fear that some of our pupils are slow to respond to familiar example. It is the exotic that appeals to them. Now if they were to be presented with some stimulus to their imagination in the form of a visitor from the great metropolis—"

"The great M'Trollops . . ." muttered Mr. O'Toole nastily. He had stood his empty glass back on the table and was now repeatedly ringing it like a bell with flicks of his middle fingernail.

Mr. Booker rose to his feet. "Let me do the honors, sir," he said to Mr. Clay.

The headmaster shook his head. "Not just at the moment." The glasses of both Mr. Hive and Mr. O'Toole were by Booker's hand; he had seen neither actually in motion. He picked them up and departed for the bar.

Mr. Clay was uncertain of whether his implied invitation had been grasped. He kept his regard steadily on Mr. Hive, who gazed back with enormous benevolence but continued to say nothing.

"I should esteem it a great favor, sir," the headmaster said at last, "if you would come along to our, ah, little symposium and possibly say a few words to the boys on the subject of your career."

60

Mr. Hive's eyes widened and shone; his mouth opened; he spread a hand over his heart. He stood up. The hand left his chest, made a couple of circular motions and remained, fingers spread, in the air. "Lead me, my dear sir," he cried, "to your siblings!"

Mr. Clay had not been prepared for such enthusiasm. He looked a fraction alarmed. "You're sure you don't mind?" he asked, hoping that Mr. Hive would soon abandon his pose.

"Mind? Certainly not! I can think of absolutely nothing that would give me greater pleasure!" Hive plonked back into his chair. His foot knocked against something hard. He looked down. It was his camera case.

"Oh, dear!" he said dolefully.

"Is something amiss?"

"Oh, dear!" Mr. Hive said again. He tasted his little finger. Mr. Clay wondered if he had been stung by a wasp. He stared at him anxiously.

"The fact is," said Mr. Hive, "that I have just remembered a most important engagement."

From Mr. O'Toole, who had been slumped in an attitude of world-weary detachment since parting with his glass, came a quiet but unmistakably derisive snigger.

"Most important," repeated Mr. Hive.

The headmaster frowned. He looked up at Mr. Booker, newly returned from the bar. "Mr. Hive says he has an engagement, Booker. You didn't mention anything about that."

"Well, I didn't know, did I? Anyway, perhaps it's not all that urgent. Eh, Mr. Hive?" He spoke without taking his eyes off the drinks that he was carefully transferring from a tray.

"The boys will be most disappointed," said Mr. Clay.

Hive took out his watch.

"Is your appointment fixed at any particular time?" Booker asked him.

"Well . . ."

"The school is very near," urged Mr. Clay. "There will, of course, be refreshments."

A guttural comment, between swallows, from O'Toole. It sounded like "Cocoa."

"You tempt me," said Mr. Hive. "Indeed you do. I remember something my old headmaster said to me during my last term at Harrow. 'Never hesitate to hand on the lamp, Hive,' he said, 'for it will burn all the more brightly if you do.' "

"How true," said Mr. Booker.

"Hodie mihi, cras tibi," solemnly added Mr. Clay.

"Puss! Puss!"

They ignored Mr. O'Toole.

"I must not be late, mind. Much depends upon my not being late."

"I think I may safely guarantee that, Mr. Hive. Half past nine—a quarter to ten at the outside. Eh, Booker?"

"We generally manage to clear things up by then, sir."

"Excellent, excellent. So what do you say, then, Mr. Hive?" The headmaster reached determinedly for his yet untasted sherry.

"Of course he will," said Mr. Booker.

Mr. Hive, after some deprecatory chuckles, downed his brandy as a gesture of good fellowship and said that, damn him, the night was young and he really thought he would. "I'm a very easily persuaded fellow," he added, suddenly and unaccountably sad.

"Incidentally . . ." Mr. Clay hesitated, drank precisely half his sherry, and went on. "I should be rather interested

62

—purely for introductory purposes—the boys, you know—to hear what your profession, ah, actually is."

"Was," corrected Mr. Hive. He was looking dreamily down the room toward the shifting white blur of the barmaid's décolletage.

"You are retired?"

"On the insistence of my doctors. Certain occupational maladies—sciatica, things like that. It was the variation in temperature, you know."

"I see," said Mr. Clay who didn't. "You mean your work took you abroad a good deal?"

"I seldom slept in my own bed."

Mr. Clay, a home-loving man, looked sympathetic. "The foreign service must entail a good deal of hardship of which ordinary people know little. It is not all balls and levees, I am sure."

Mr. Hive frowned. "I don't remember any levees."

The headmaster felt a twinge of annoyance. The man was being singularly obtuse. But diplomats doubtless were so by nature. And they were, of course, bound by the Official Secrets Act. It would not do to drive the man, by too direct a catechism, into a blank denial of his profession. That would not be fair to the boys.

"Did you serve many years in the, ah—"

"For nearly a quarter of a century," replied Mr. Hive with a promptness and a warmth that immediately dispelled the headmaster's fear of overfishing. "This would have been my silver jubilee year."

"Fancy that!" said Booker.

O'Toole's fingernail had begun to ring his glass once more.

Mr. Clay pursued his advantage. "I should be surprised if in so long a period you have not received some tokens of,

63

ah, official recognition of your . . ." Again he left at the end of the sentence a space that he hoped Mr. Hive would fill in.

"Various little things have come my way, you know."

Mr. Clay leaned forward and assumed the expression of one who has just recalled what might prove a valuable clue.

"I seem to remember," he said slowly, "having seen your name before somewhere. In, I think, the *Times* newspaper . . ." He watched Mr. Hive's face. "It could have been the Court Circular column. . . ."

"Court?" echoed Mr. Hive eagerly.

"Yes."

"Oh, very probably."

"A citation, I fancy . . ." Mr. Clay felt intoxicated by his own mendacity.

Mr. Hive smiled at his finger ends, then much more warmly at Mr. Clay.

"You can have no idea," he said, "of how gratifying it is to a mere toiler in the vineyard to hear that his wine has earned good report."

"Then I may tell the boys, may I not, that their, ah, guest of honor, has been cited, ah . . ."

"By all means, my dear sir! Forty-seven times."

6

IN the middle of one of the smaller lawns at the back of the Palgroves' home was a circular wall of concrete, about three feet in diameter and a little less than three feet high, from which two posts rose to support a steeply pitched roof. The posts also carried a crank, set in a roller from which hung a chain. The wall was brightly painted in imitation of brick. The little roof, held up like an umbrella by the posts, was in fact plastic, but it was the same jolly red as the wall and from a distance might have been taken as tile. The whole contrivance, of course, was intended to resemble an old country wellhead—a "wishing well," in fact, according to the catalog of the firm of garden-furniture manufacturers from which Mrs. Palgrove had bought it a couple of years before.

Around the well, set in the grass, were several large plastic toadstools, colored in rich browns and reds and yellows. Upon one of them squatted a giant frog, very droll, very lifelike. Lifelike, too, were the dwarfs, modeled in attitudes of fey mischief, that completed the tableau.

Mrs. Palgrove paused on her way from the house and watched the effect of the setting sun upon the little plastic community. Against the long shadow cast by the well across the grass, the dwarfs' scarlet caps gleamed like peppers.

Rodney ran past her and toured the toadstools, sniffing them and making equitable bestowal of urine. "Bad boy! Nasty!" called Mrs. Palgrove mechanically and quite without rancor. Rodney ignored her.

She went up to the well. It was filled almost to the brim with water. In the depths glided thin orange shapes. Mrs. Palgrove took from the pocket of her coat a small jar with perforated lid and shook white crumbs on the surface. The crumbs spread out and began to sink slowly. A pair, three, four goldfish came mouthing up to the food. Mrs. Palgrove unconsciously imitated a fish's ingesting pout as she watched them suck in the descending, disintegrating fragments.

"Good boys! Clever boys!"

The last of the sun had slid from the lawns and was climbing the beech hedge at the far side of the garden. In the chilly, deepening shade the dwarfs and the toadstools and the frog reverted to lifeless shapes, scarcely identifiable. The vermilion of the dummy well became the color of dried blood. A cold breeze rustled the leaves of the chestnut trees.

Mrs. Palgrove bade the goldfish good night and went back to the house. Rodney was there already, painstakingly gnawing the tapestry cover off one of the chairs in the dining room.

"Bad boy! Naughty!" She left Rodney to his depredations and went into the lounge, switching on the light. This came from a set of candlelike lamps fixed to a varnished oak frame suspended from the ceiling by four chains. The frame only just cleared Mrs. Palgrove's head. She knelt

66

and switched on the electric fire; it simulated glowing coals.

Looking around for the evening paper, she spotted it on the table by the French window. Her husband had left it, racing page uppermost, propped against a model of a Spanish galleon. The model was complete in every detail; it had been a wedding present, and Mrs. Palgrove supposed it to be fragile and valuable. Carefully she removed the newspaper and took it over to the settee, glancing on the way at the clock on the mantelpiece. It was twenty minutes past seven.

At a quarter to eight, Mrs. Palgrove folded the paper and added it to others in a rack by the fireplace. The rack was in the form of a pair of shields embossed with heraldic designs and clipped back to back. She walked soundlessly across the thick, silver-gray carpet patterned here and there with little yellow maps (of Rodney's devising) and let down the front flap of a writing cabinet. Then, uncasing the portable typewriter that had been stood beneath the cabinet, she put it on the extended flap and drew up a chair.

She wound into the typewriter a sheet of gray paper headed with the words FOUR FOOT HAVEN in large green capitals above a printed line drawing of two dogs, one in lace cap and apron, the other bespectacled and smoking a pipe, seated in humanized postures of relaxation on either side of a fireplace.

Mrs. Palgrove began to type, addressing the letter to Miss L. E. C. Teatime, Secretary, Flaxborough and Eastern Counties Charities Alliance, 31 St. Anne's Gate, Flaxborough.

Dear Madam . . .

She considered a moment and went on, striking the keys slowly but with deliberation and accuracy.

67

The committee of my society considered at its last meeting a certain incident of which you must be aware and which took place on the 14th inst. I refer to the breaking open after dark of the haven kennels ("Rover-Holme") and the introduction of an unauthorized animal, which the committee has reason to believe was an "unwell" lady dog. The result was that "Rover-Holme" was empty the next day, and we have had to send members with cars as far away as Chalmsbury to collect our poor animals. More than twenty are still missing, and it may well be that they have fallen into the hands of the vivisectionists. I would not have somebody's conscience for all the tea in China.

THE POLICE HAVE BEEN INFORMED.

Now what my committee wishes to be known is that we are not going to be intimidated by ANYBODY, *no matter what that anybody may do next. The Four-Foot Haven is a truly* INDEPENDENT *body, and it refuses to be swallowed up by a big organization using ruthless and un-English methods.*

Mrs. Palgrove paused and read back what she had written. She pondered a full minute before adding the final paragraph.

It may interest you to know that certain information has reached me privately concerning the disposal of funds raised not a hundred miles from here in the name of so-called charity. I am reluctant to pass this information to the authorities, but I shall not hesitate to do so if the need arises. "If the shoe fits . . . etc." Need I say more?
Yours very sincerely,

Again she sat in thought, staring at the sheet of paper before her. Then, in sudden resolve, she released it from the machine, put aside the carbon copy and added her signature in large angular script. She addressed an envelope, affixed a stamp that she took from a supply in a flat tin box, folded the letter and sealed it within the envelope.

Three minutes later Mrs. Palgrove was walking energetically along Brompton Gardens toward the mailbox at the Heston Lane corner.

The careers symposium was held in the physics lecture theater of the grammar school. The room was in one of the oldest parts of the building. Its loftiness, its row of narrow, pseudo-Gothic windows, its oak and cast-iron desks radiating in rising tiers from a huge demonstration bench all testified to mid-Victorian zeal for the propagation of science.

Some three dozen boys had distributed themselves, mainly in the four back rows. Aware that the occasion was ostensibly one of voluntary attendance, they were in a mood to extract from it such entertainment as they could. Their headmaster sensed it as soon as he entered the room and led his guests to the line of chairs that had been prepared for them on a dais behind the demonstration bench. "Watch them, Booker," he murmured. "I fear persiflage."

With much scuffling of feet and several extravagant sighs intended to sound symptomatic of premature aging brought about by too many afterschool obligations, the boys rose.

Mr. Clay waited for silence, then told them they might sit. They did so as if they had just come in from an obstacle course.

The headmaster went quickly through his routine explanation of what a careers symposium was supposed to achieve and then proceeded to introduce those whom he termed "our visitors from the world of effort and accomplishment."

69

He indicated first Mr. Ernest Hideaway, real estate agent and appraiser.

Mr. Hideaway, a merry-looking baldy with big, floppy lips and eyes that constantly monitored his audience as if on the watch for bids, was a familiar performer at these functions. The boys waited for him to play his joke. As soon as his name was mentioned, he produced from his pocket a gavel and rapped with it three times on the bench. "Sold to the gentleman in the back row!" cried Mr. Hideaway. There was noisy applause. The headmaster smiled icily and held up his hand.

"Next I should like to welcome Inspector Purbright of the Borough Constabulary, who has very kindly taken time off from his many pressing duties so that his advice may be available to us this evening."

Some of the more sanguine watched for the inspector to outdo Mr. Hideaway by whipping out a truncheon, but he simply smiled and continued to lean back with folded arms.

"A no less distinguished representative of the law, though in another field, is our old friend Mr. Justin Scorpe." Mr. Clay turned and nodded to a man with a long wooden face, whose chief occupation seemed to be putting on and taking off a pair of massive black-framed spectacles. The solicitor acknowledged Mr. Clay's tribute by looking gravely up at the ceiling and clearing his throat—an action which made his Adam's apple look like a bouncing golf ball.

"From the sphere of commerce we have with us Mr. Barnstaple."

There rose to his feet a frail man with thinning, untidy hair and very bright blue eyes. He made a stooping bob to his audience, flapped his hands once or twice, and sat down after glancing apologetically at Mr. Clay.

We had hoped, as you know, to be favored with the presence of Mr. Behan [the headmaster pronounced it Bee-hahn] of the Flaxborough Timber Corporation, but unfortunately he was called away on important business, and Mr. Barnstaple kindly agreed to stand in for him. Mr. Barnstaple is Mr. Behan's accountant."

This explanation having been trotted out for what it was worth—clearly very little, in Mr. Clay's opinion— the headmaster paused, clasped his hands in front of him, and gazed into the top left-hand corner of the room.

"And now," he said, "I should like to introduce to you boys a very special guest. He is the gentleman you see sitting next to our ever-helpful friend from the Ministry of Labour, Mr. O'Toole. I refer to Mr. Mortimer Hive."

Dutiful hand-clapping almost, but not quite, drowned the contribution by a few wits of the lower sixth of a high buzzing sound, as of angry bees. Mr. Booker looked up sharply toward its origin and made a penciled note on the back of an envelope.

"Mr. Hive," the headmaster went on, "is from London."

"Big deal!" breathed the youth employment coordinator. Purbright glanced across at him and thought he looked more like a recumbent beachcomber than ever.

"And when I say he is from London, I do not think I betray any interests of, ah, national security by telling you that his work—from which he has now retired—was of a highly significant nature." Mr. Clay half turned. "I am right, am I not, Mr. Hive?"

Hive grinned prodigiously and somewhat to Mr. Clay's surprise hooked the fingers of both hands together above his head in the manner of a triumphant prizefighter.

The boys, too, were surprised—but pleasantly so. The gesture, like Mr. Hideaway's gavel beating, held prospect of light relief. One boy subjected Mr. Hive to long and

71

careful scrutiny and then, with all the certitude of the expert, declared to his companions: "He's pissed." Hopes ran very high.

"Before I invite you to put questions to members of our panel, a word of explanation to those boys—and I see there are one or two of them—who have not attended one of these little functions before. You may ask these good gentlemen anything you like, provided"—Mr. Clay paused portentously—"provided, I say, that the question is relevant to the matter of employment. What I do not want—NOT want to hear—and I assure you that Mr. Booker will not want to hear them either—are questions of a fatuous or, ah, provocative nature. You know what I mean. And Mr. Booker knows what I mean. Very well, then. First boy . . ."

And Mr. Clay sat down.

Purbright, whose first visit to the school in an advisory capacity this was, tried to, think what he might be asked. *Please, sir how do I become a detective?* That wouldn't be too bad. A short summary of recruitment procedure—branches of the force—promotion. He could cope with that. *Please, sir, is there an examination for getting into the police? Please, sir, is it all right for anyone who has to wear glasses? Please, sir . . .*

"Please, sir, could the inspector tell us what his job is worth? Salary, I mean, sir. And extras."

The questioner was a grave-faced boy of fifteen. Purbright thought he looked about twenty-four.

Purbright said: "Well . . ." which seemed as good a beginning as any. Then he saw that the headmaster's hand was raised, flat and prohibitory.

"No, Rawlings. I do not think we should frame our questions in quite such a personal—directly personal—form. If, as you very reasonably might, you wish to learn the scale

72

of emoluments in the police force, I feel sure that our good friend Mr. O'Toole will be pleased to provide you with the appropriate literature. Oh, and Rawlings, I am confident that Inspector Purbright will not contradict me when I say that police officers in this country do not receive, ah, perquisites."

The boy stared archly at Mr. Clay. "I didn't mean *bribes*, sir. Not in the sense that you—"

"That will do, Rawlings." Mr. Clay resumed his seat with the uncomfortable suspicion that he had been maneuvered into slandering somebody.

The ensuing silence was pierced by a thin, tinny sound. Music. Mr. Booker stiffened and looked toward the back rows of desks. The sound rose suddenly to a crescendo, then was cut off. Some of the boys at the back craned their necks at one another and shuffled to close ranks.

Booker left his seat and, crouching, crept silently up the side aisle. Those on the platform pretended not to notice.

"Next question," called Mr. Clay. He waited, rigidly facing front.

Booker eased his way along the back row as far as the fourth desk. He held out his hand. The plump, nervous boy who was vainly trying to conceal a transistor radio set between his knees gazed at the hand in mute disbelief, as though it were unattached and had arrived there of its own volition.

"Come along," said Mr. Booker very quietly. The fingers of the hand curled, inviting sacrifice.

The boy swallowed. "But it's not mine, sir. It's Wagstaff's. I was just looking at it."

The hand remained. It was very still. It looked a strong and patient hand. Somewhere else in the room a question was being asked about sawmills.

The plump boy surrendered the radio that was not

73

his own, and Mr. Booker went creeping back to his seat. Purbright noticed that he was smiling.

"Please, sir, can Mr. Scorpe tell us if soliciting is a good profession, sir?"

This was asked by a youth with an expression so innocent that Purbright guessed he had been coaxed or coerced by his fellows. The fact that he wore rather prominent glasses—in parody, as it were, of Mr. Scorpe's—could also have influenced his selection as spokesman.

If the insult had registered, the lawyer gave no sign. He nodded very solemnly, yo-yoed his Adam's apple once or twice, and spoke.

"The question, as I understand it, is this: Does the calling of the solicitor [he pronounced the *or* part most sonorously] bring rewards consistent with his dignity? Financially, I regret to say it does not. . . ."

"Oh, Christ!" came distinctly from the direction of Mr. O'Toole.

"By which I mean to say," continued Mr. Scorpe, "that his is a grossly undervalued profession and that the public receives from him a service of immeasurably greater worth than his mere fee. It would, however, be invidious to pursue such a theme without pointing out . . ."

Mr. Scorpe went on a lot longer and evinced many impressive arguments. What they boiled down to was that lawyers alone were pernurious in a pampered world.

The boys were unsympathetic. What they had overheard from parents in the matter of Mr. Scorpe's bills, particularly those relating to house purchase, had created the image of a licensed extortioner. Now he had simply made the impression worse by boring the pants off them.

The headmaster, too, had grown edgy. Time was running out and his capture of the evening, the illustrious Mr. Hive, had not yet been given a cue. Mr. Clay felt like

74

an impresario whose leading tenor was being kept off the boards by lack of a work permit.

But Mr. Scorpe's tendentious recital rolled at last to an end. Before he could slip in an encore, a tall youth with an incipient mustache hastily expressed interest in auctioneering, and Mr. Hideaway took over. He told several stories of his trade in a fruity, quick-fire voice and with a wealth of marketplace rhetoric. They were climaxed by a tale of a farm laborer from Gosby Vale who had bartered for a motorcycle his wife and five pounds of kidney beans.

To Purbright the story was already familiar. He had heard it, indeed, as a complaint from the man who had parted with the motorcycle. "You'd think the mean bugger'd 've put 'em in a bag," he had said of the beans.

The headmaster, who had made a mental note not to invite Mr. Hideaway again, looked at his watch. It was ten past nine. He hoped no one would now ask anything about timber mills or accountancy; that Barnstaple person looked the sort to meander on for hours without getting a proper answer out. He stole a glance at his prize guest, then primped his mouth in dismay.

Mr. Hive was fast asleep.

The boy Rawlings had made the same observation. He raised his hand.

"Please, sir, do you think the gentleman from London could tell us something about employment prospects in his own line or business—whatever that is, sir?"

"Thank you, Rawlings." *Blast the boy! A born troublemaker, if ever there was one.* "Ah, Mr. Hive . . ."

For several seconds, every boy in the room watched the contented sleep mask. Like certain magistrates and all judges, Mr. Hive had the art of quitting consciousness gracefully. He did not loll. He did not snore. His eyes were

75

closed, certainly, but in that placid manner one associates with listening to music or enjoying the scent of flowers.

"Um, ah, Mr. Hive . . ."

There brushed past the sleeper's elegant, full-fashioned mustache a light sigh.

The headmaster tried to catch the eye of Mr. O'Toole by making discreet little pecking gestures in the air with finger and thumb. Eventually O'Toole got the message. He grinned and rammed his elbow into Mr. Hive. "Hey, sailor! You're wanted on deck!"

Hive's reaction was as dramatic as any of the audience could have wished. It was also—in Mr. Clay's view, at any rate—quite inexplicable.

The man reared to his feet and stood leaning slightly forward and sideways with hands raised to the level of his face, one above the other. As he squinted between the hands, one eye closed, he cried: "Watch the birdie, dear lady! You, too, sir. And no embarrassment, I beg!"

The boys laughed. Some clapped as well. Mr. Hive lowered his arms. He looked mildly surprised.

"What did I tell you?" remarked the boy who had diagnosed intoxication. His neighbor slipped him a toffee in tribute.

Mr. Clay waited for the excitement to subside. The shrewder side of his intelligence had already grasped the simple cause of Mr. Hive's curious behavior. It urged him to bring the proceedings to a close there and then in a firm and dignified manner. But Mr. Clay was a proud and, in certain respects, a daring man.

He forced as broad a smile as the tightness of his skin would allow. "I see that Mr. Hive would have us believe that it was in the photographic field that he achieved his reputation. Ah, but we know—do we not?—that one does not receive official citation for taking snapshots!"

Hive laughed so heartily at this that he had difficulty in keeping his balance. It was only the timely aid of Mr. Barnstaple, who reached up and grabbed his arm, that prevented his falling from the dais.

He stopped laughing and stared thoughtfully at Mr. Barnstaple's hand. Then he looked at the boys, at Inspector Purbright and Mr. Hideaway, at Mr. Clay. He frowned and bent close to the ear of Mr. O'Toole.

"Who are all those boys?" he whispered.

"What boys?"

"Boys. Bundles of boys . . . My God, it isn't a choir, is it?"

There stirred suddenly in Mr. O'Toole some sympathetic instinct, a sort of drinker's loyalty. He breathed rapid explanation—"School—speeches—usual guff—you—*now*"—and with a heave under Hive's elbow set him in a more or less perpendicular pose.

Mr. Hive was so grateful for enlightenment concerning what was immediately expected of him that he pushed from his mind the still unsolved riddle of how he had come to wake up in a school, of all places. He would puzzle that out later; it was probably something to do with the case. One thing was sure—and he smiled wryly at the thought—there was always some new demand on a detective's versatility.

"Boys! . . . No [a roguishly wagged finger]—gentlemen! When your headmaster [a bow to Purbright] was kind enough to ask me to come along and present your prizes today, do you know the first thing I said to him? The very first thing I said? You don't. No. Never mind. [An up-brushing of Mr. Hive's mustache with splayed fingers.] You see, in the game of . . . Ah. Now, then. Now. There's one thing that's all . . . All-important, this thing. When your headmaster was kind enough to ask me to come along,

77

he said, in the game of life. No, no, no—*I* said. Me. Winning not the main thing. These prizes, you see. Some people don't want. Get em. Don't want 'em. More'n they bargain for. When your headmaster . . . no, said that. [Another rummage in the mustache.] People with prizes didn't want in the game of life—sent for me. Hive, they said . . . Important people, mind. Ooooh, very important. Rubbed shoulders with aristocracy. [A sly, lopsided smirk.] Not just shoulders, either. Never mind that. Hive, they said, don't want it—sick of it—want another one. For crissake, get rid. And that was it, gentlemen. Tokens of appreciation to show. [Groping into his watch pocket.] Oh, and beautiful memories. Tell you one when your headmaster kind enough to ask. Tell you one. Ever seen a birthmark—know what birthmark is? Course you do . . . Ever seen a birthmark exactly same shape as Statue 'f Liberty, torch an' all? Haven't, have you? Not torch an' all. I have, though. In the game of life . . . no, not game, profession. Profession. I'll tell you kind enough to ask. On Lady Felicity Hoop's left buttock. [A squinting search of memory.] No. As you were. *Right* buttock. Right, yes—torch an' all. Lovely woman. Dead now."

Mr. Hive bowed his head, as if to inaugurate a two minutes' silence. The headmaster seized his chance. He hastened around to the front of the demonstration bench, commanded the nearest boy to open the door and told the assembly to file out quietly.

As the boys shuffled from the room, they glanced secretively and with awe at the figure of Mr. Hive, who, oblivious of their departure, still swayed in silent tribute to the late Lady Felicity.

One boy hung back. It was Wagstaff. He climbed onto the platform and made his way to Mr. Booker.

"Please, sir, may I have my transistor back now, sir?"

"Transistor? What transistor, boy?"

"That one, sir. It's mine."

Purbright watched him point to the set that Booker had laid on the bench before him.

"That," said Booker, "was in the possession of Holly. He was misbehaving and suffered the penalty. It is confiscated."

"But it isn't Holly's, sir. He was just looking at it. It's mine."

"It is confiscated."

"But, sir—"

"I really don't see that I can put the matter any more plainly, Wagstaff. We all must pay for our transgressions. If you feel that you are the victim of injustice—and I cannot understand why you should—you will just have to thrash it out with your friend Holly."

The boy stood a few moments longer in tearful perplexity, but Booker had swiveled around in his chair and was now staring thoughtfully at Mr. Hive, who had abandoned his posture of grief and was searching for something. Wagstaff took a last lingering look at his radio and slouched away.

"Where's my camera?" demanded Mr. Hive, a little sobered by alarm.

Mr. Hideaway and Mr. Barnstaple looked under chairs. Mr. O'Toole shrugged and picked at one of his back teeth with his little fingernail. "*Now* what's he want?" the headmaster inquired irritably of Mr. Booker.

Hive began to feel through his pockets.

"He says he's lost his camera."

"I saw no camera," said Mr. Clay. "He was carrying a sort of suitcase when we were in that hotel."

"He hasn't got it now."

"Well, I cannot help that. He must be gotten out of the

79

school. I rely on you to see to it. Oh, and Booker . . . a word with you before assembly in the morning, if you wouldn't mind."

Mr. Clay turned away and put a hand on Purbright's arm. "A little refreshment before you leave, Inspector? One of Mrs. Wilson's excellent concoctions is doubtless awaiting us in the common room."

The headmaster herded into the corridor all his guests save Mr. Hive. He, watched by Booker from the doorway, continued for several minutes to wander up and down, peering under desks.

"You must have left it in the pub."

Hive stood still. "Pub?" He looked immensely grateful. Even the most mystifying losses could, he knew, be made good if only one could find again the right pub.

"The Three Crowns," said Booker. "Just around the corner. I'll show you."

At the gates of the school, Booker pointed to a streetlamp about twenty yards away that marked the opening of a narrow lane. "In that lane. You'll see it as soon as you get to the corner."

Hive strode off resolutely toward his objective. Some small trouble with one of his legs gave him a tendency to veer off course, but he corrected this at intervals so that his progress was a series of arcs. Booker watched him reach the corner lamp, swing around it twice and shoot off at a nicely judged tangent into the lane's mouth.

The barmaid at the Three Crowns showed great concern on hearing of the loss of Mr. Hive's case. She even left the bar long enough to search beneath every table, parting the customers' legs as though they were stems of undergrowth. Hive hovered close by and gained some compensation from his new and very advantageous viewpoint of the girl's bosom. Of the camera, however, there was no sign.

Hive loitered only for one double brandy before making his way back to the school gates. These he was chagrined to find locked. He shook them and shouted several times, but to no avail. He tried to climb one of the gates and succeeded only in getting one shoe wedged in some scrollwork. By the time he had unlaced it, withdrawn his foot, extricated the shoe and put it on again, all notion of getting back into the school had evaporated. Camera or no camera, the task of the night was waiting to be done. A man of resource could be disarmed but never dismayed. Have at them, Hive! Forward to . . . to . . . Ah, yes—Hambourne Dyke. Forward to Hambourne Dyke! (First left after level crossing, second cottage, bedroom at back, window by water barrel.) Moment of truth. Moment of Hive!

He lurched from the gates and returned at a lumbering, weaving trot to the cobbled yard of the Three Crowns.

For nearly ten minutes the customers within heard the spasmodic labor of a starter motor gradually become slower and feebler as it vainly contended with the engine of an elderly car from which the distributor had been removed.

7

"LOOKS like number three. It looks *very* much like number three."

Such was Sergeant Malley's comment—made not gleefully but with a certain sense of relief—when the constable on switchboard duty rang up to tell him that a lady had just been found dead in Brompton Gardens. Fate, the sergeant knew from his long experience, worked in triples. Waiting for the completion of each set always made him fidgety; it was like straining an ear to catch the note necessary for a perfect cadence.

"Not likely to be a natural cause, is it?"

"I don't think so, Sergeant. The woman who rang in said something about the body being in some water."

"What, in a bath, you mean?"

"No . . ." The constable's voice faltered. "In a well, actually."

"A well! In Brompton Gardens?"

"That's what I thought she said. Harper and Fairclough have gone over there. I expect they'll be able to tell you more about it."

"Have you got the name?"

"It's a lady called Mrs. Palgrove."

"Good lord," said Malley, "it isn't!"

He went along at once to inspector Purbright's office.

"Guess who's been found down a well."

Purbright looked up wearily from a file that was beginning to show signs of long and fruitless perusal. "Some bloody charity organizer, I expect. That would be all I needed."

For a moment Malley gaped, as at a miraculously speaking statue. Then his expression was restored to plump, bland normality tinged with disappointment. "Oh, so you've heard already."

"Heard? Heard what?"

"This business about a woman in a well. It's Mrs. Palgrove. 'Pally' Palgrove's missus. Brompton Gardens."

"Good God!"

"Well, when you said—"

"That? No, I was just being . . . Here, you're sure about this?" Purbright was on his feet.

"We've only had a phone report up to now. It seems right, though. A couple of the lads have gone to the house."

The inspector pulled his coat straight and picked up a packet of cigarettes from the desk. "I think we'd better join them. I'll want Sergeant Love as well. See if he's in the canteen, will you, Bill?"

Purbright drove the car. It was one of a pair reserved for journeys within the borough boundaries. Both were black, stately, and secondhand. The upholstery was real leather. Gray silk blinds with fringes could be drawn down over the rear windows. The highly burnished radiator of each car was surmounted by a temperature gauge like a little monument. Among the Flaxborough policemen the cars were known as the Widows. Purbright had chosen the

83

one less favored by the chief constable; its smell of Yorkshire terrier was not so strong.

Sergeant Love occupied the passenger seat next to Purbright. Sergeant Malley filled the back.

The inspector said to Love: "You'd better tell Bill here about the names you got yesterday from Dawson's. He's already seen the letter that was sent around."

Love spoke over the back of his seat. "I asked them who'd been buying that kind of writing paper—you know, that gray stuff. They could only think of one person who'd bought any recently. Mrs. Palgrove. She got it regularly."

"Oh, aye?" Malley was scraping out the bowl of his pipe with an enormous clasp knife. He blew through the pipe experimentally, then pulled away the stem and held it up to one eye.

"Well, then?" urged Love a little irritably. He did not like wasting dramatic announcements on people who messed about with pipes all the time

"Very interesting," Malley said.

Love faced forward again. For a while he stared through the windshield without speaking.

"It could be," Purbright said to him, "that you've put us onto something important, Sid."

Love glowed.

The car pursued its slow, dignified course up Heston Lane. It looked rather like a straggler from a funeral procession that had been cut off at traffic lights. Indeed, as it turned at last into the driveway of Dunroamin, a woman in the house opposite called upstairs to her bedridden mother: "It's right about Mrs. Palgrove, then. The undertaker's just come."

Purbright parked the car near the main door of the house. He rang the bell. After a fairly long interval, it was answered by a squat, middle-aged woman. Although she

84

wore an apron, she had kept on her hat. It gave her the air of a helper prepared for flight at the first sign of fresh disaster. And she clearly regarded the appearance of the three policemen as just that.

"You'll have to excuse me. I've got to get along home now." She began to unfasten the apron.

"You will be Mrs.—"

"George. Mrs. George. I help here. But I'll have to be getting back."

"I see. We shan't keep you long, Mrs. George. There are just a couple of things I'd like to ask you, though."

They were now inside the entrance hall. Love looked around approvingly and rocked a little on his heels to test the elasticity of the carpet. Catching Malley's eye, he raised his brows and pouted; Love was a great fancier of house interiors.

The woman opened a closet door and hung the apron inside.

"Was it you who telephoned us this morning, Mrs. George?"

She nodded.

"Then I wonder if you'd mind telling me exactly what you found when you arrived. You'd come to help with the housework, had you?"

"That's right. I come every day and give a hand. This morning the bus was a bit late, but even so, I don't think it was quite nine o'clock when I got here. I went around to the kitchen door, expecting it to be open as usual . . ."

"Open?"

"Well, not open—unlocked, I mean. Anyway, it wasn't, so I knocked a few times and waited about a while, but nobody came, so I went to the big door and rang the bell. Still nobody answered. I couldn't hear a sound inside and I thought, funny, because Mrs. Palgrove hadn't said anything the day before about going away, which she would have done, of course. Well, I thought I'd better give them a few minutes just in case, so I started to walk about a bit outside and look at the flowers. Of course it was then I—I—"

Mrs. George felt instinctively for her apron. Tears had started afresh from her already reddened eyes. She rubbed them with the back of her hand, which she then pressed to her mouth.

Purbright put an arm around her shoulders and led her to a chair by the foot of the stairs. Love and Malley left, at a sign from the inspector, to join their colleagues in the garden.

"Yes, Mrs. George?"

She raised a face lined and puffy with distress. "Yes . . . well . . . I mean, there she was. Sort of doubled over the wall of that well thing. Half of her outside, the other half inside. Right in the water. Oh, arms, shoulders, head— right under. And them fishes . . . swimming about around her hair. In and out . . ."

Mrs. George looked down at her skirt and pressed her knuckles into it. She swayed slightly backward and forward.

"Did you pull her out of the water?"

She shook her head. "I didn't seem able to manage it. She's quite a big woman, you know."

"It was very sensible of you to telephone."

"I tried to get her out. I tried all ways. It was no good, though. I mean, people are a lot heavier than they look, aren't they, especially when they're lying awkward. Well, anyway, I just couldn't. So I ran down to the phone at the corner. It seemed best, I mean. . . ."

"Of course. By the way, how did you get into the house eventually?"

"Get in?"

86

"You did open the door to us."

"Yes. One of the policemen who came found a window open, and he got through. He said it would be all right."

"I suppose Mr. Palgrove is away from home, is he?"

"I don't know. I mean, he's not here now, and it's not usual for him to leave for business until, oh, an hour or more after I arrive. The other policemen wanted to know, and I told them the same. They'd most likely know at his office. I mean, you could try his office."

"I could, couldn't I? All right, Mrs. George, there's no reason why you should stay any longer. You've been most patient."

He helped her to her feet, then opened the door. As she trotted dumpily past him, she gave a nervous little smile of farewell, followed by a brief, fearful glance toward the distant policemen grouped about a shrouded shape in the grass.

"Dead for hours," Love announced when Purbright came up. He drew back the blanket that Harper had brought from the house.

The inspector looked down at the big, vacuous face in which the eyes were just two dark dots. The wet hair, close-clinging as a cap but with a few unraveled strands wandering down over forehead and cheek, seemed too sparse, too lank, to be a woman's. This dissolution of sexual identity, furthered by the laxity of the cheeks and the jaw, was made more shocking still by the survival of the woman's last application of lipstick and eye shadow, now garish daubs amidst the water-bleached flesh.

"How long do you think the doctor will be?"

Harper looked at his watch. "Any time now, sir. It's Doctor Fergusson from the General. We couldn't get hold of Reynolds."

"You've tried to contact the husband?"

The uniformed man, Fairclough, coughed and gave Harper a glance before replying.

"We haven't had much luck, sir. There was only the cleaner here when we arrived, and she seemed to think he was away from home. I rang his firm, but—"

"That's Can-flax, isn't it?"

"Yes, sir. I rang them straightaway, but he wasn't there. They said he doesn't usually turn up before ten. I called a bit later, when his secretary had come in, and she said he'd arranged to go to Leicester last night."

"When does she expect him back?"

"Sometime this morning, she thinks."

"All right. Well, at least we know why he isn't here. Look, Mr. Harper, you'd better get over to Can-flax and wait around in case Palgrove goes straight to his office. Break things to him gently and tell him there'll be somebody here waiting."

Sergeant Love was going slowly around the well, examining it. He tried to turn the crank. It was fixed, make-believe like the bucket and the few links of chain and all the rest.

"What a swizzl!" said Love. Fairclough eyed him with disapproval.

"You didn't think it was real, did you, Sid?" Purbright perched himself carefully on the edge of the wall and peered into the water. The fish, agitated, crossed and re-crossed in sudden darts and swoops.

"How do you think it happened?" Purbright asked.

"She must have leaned too far over, I suppose." Love was still suffering disenchantment.

Malley, who had been silently filling his pipe, stowed the tobacco pouch into the breast pocket of his already over-occupied tunic and lowered himself to a kneeling position against the wall. He craned forward experimentally.

88

"She'd have a job," he said. "Bloody hard on the belly, this edge is."

"Supposing your hands slipped now, Bill. Wouldn't your head and perhaps your shoulders go under?"

"Aye, they might, just for a second. But I could easily enough yank them out again. Look—as long as you've got the weight of your legs on this side of the wall, you're anchored. You can get your head up any time you like, then push yourself back—like this." With a heave and some very labored breathing, Malley lumbered to his feet.

The demonstration, though ponderous, seemed reasonable. Purbright nodded. "Then why," he said a little later, "didn't Mrs. Palgrove push herself back?" He turned to Fairclough. "It was only the upper part of her body that was in the water, wasn't it?"

"That's right, sir. The lady was sort of jackknifed across the wall. One half each side." He took a step nearer. "I could show you if you like, sir."

"Oh, no, you needn't do that, Mr. Fairclough. I quite see what you mean." Purbright nearly added a pleasantry about the superfluity of another inquest, Malley having collected his set, but decided not to risk hurting Fairclough's feelings.

Malley put a match to his pipe. "There's only one explanation that I can think of."

"Heart attack," put in Love, eager to score.

Malley shrugged and puffed smoke. "It does happen. And she looks overweight, poor soul."

Purbright tried not to look too pointedly at the considerable girth of the coroner's officer, but Love was less delicate. He stared at Malley's belly with pretended alarm.

"Don't worry, son," Malley told him. "I don't go out feeding goldfish in the middle of the night."

The inspector frowned. "Middle of the night?"

"Well, it must have been dark, anyway. The lads saw this at the bottom and raked it out." Malley pulled away a corner of the blanket to reveal a battery lantern. When Purbright picked it up, water dripped from its casing.

"Was there anything else down there?"

"We only saw that flashlight," Fairclough said, "but we didn't make what you might call a proper search, sir."

"No. Naturally." Purbright looked back toward the road. He had glimpsed flashes of blue light through the leaves. "Here's the ambulance now."

Accompanying the two uniformed ambulance attendants who marched woodenly across the lawn linked by their stretcher was an alert little man with a bronzed bald head. He came tut-tutting up to Purbright and said, well, he didn't know, he was sure. The inspector was put in mind of an electrician impatiently responding to the call of some amateurish fool who'd blown a fuse.

Doctor Fergusson set down his bag, knelt and peeled back the blanket. He tutted a few more times and set fingers lightly exploring. "Dearie me, dearie, dearie me!" Then, over his shoulder to Purbright: "What the dickens had she been up to?"

"I really wouldn't know, Doctor."

"You wouldn't. No. Ay-ay-ay-ay . . . Well, there it is." He rose, brushing his trousers, and made a sign to the ambulance men.

"Who'll be doing the P.M., Doctor?" Malley asked.

"Oh, Reynolds, probably. If he's not too tied up. Otherwise . . ." Fergusson shrugged and picked up his bag. "I'll be off, then, gentlemen." And he was.

"It's all right," Malley confided to Purbright. "Fergie'll do it the minute they unload the wagon. He's like a kid in the bath when he gets into that path lab." He patted his cap more firmly on his head and turned to follow the retreating stretcher party.

The inspector told Fairclough to remain where he was for the time being. He and Love began to walk back to the house.

They had almost reached the door when something small and hairy rocketed out of the shrubbery, yapped hysterically for several seconds, then attached itself by its teeth to Love's leg. It was Rodney.

Love hopped, kicked and swore simultaneously and with a vigor of which Purbright had not suspected him capable, but the dog hung on. The inspector came to his aid. He gripped Rodney's neck just behind the clamped jaws, prised the animal away, and held it at arm's length.

"Now what do I do with it, for God's sake?"

Love was too busy massaging his calf to offer suggestions. Purbright looked about him helplessly, a Perseus wondering how to dispose safely of the head of some diminutive Gorgon. He glanced up. Almost immediately overhead was the open casement window of one of the bedrooms. It seemed to offer the only hope. He made two preparatory swings, then immediately sent his arm around again, shutting his eyes and releasing his grip at the same moment. He heard a *diminuendo* of yapping as Rodney went aloft, succeeded by sustained but mercifully muffled sounds of frenzy.

Love, who had not seen the manner of his deliverance, straightened up and stared incredulously at the inspector. "Where the hell has it gone?"

Purbright assumed his modest-athlete expression. "Into orbit, I fancy." He pushed open the front door and went into the house.

8

"IS that Dover?" asked Mr. Hive. There was no immediate reply. He heard the rackety noise transmitted by a telephone when it is laid down on something hard. Then there came other sounds, one of them suggestive of a closing door.

"Hastings, I suppose?"

"Correct," said Mr. Hive.

"Look, I did tell you not to ring at lunchtime. It's not convenient."

"Yes, I'm sorry, but I thought you'd want to be told as soon as possible about something rather disastrous."

"How do you mean?"

"Well—last night, naturally. I mean, contretemps is scarcely the word. As if it weren't enough to have my camera stolen and my car sabotaged—"

"Camera? Car?"

"My dear sir, you don't know the half of it. I still don't know what they did to the car, but it certainly wouldn't start. I just had to abandon it and set off for that benighted, blasted cottage on foot."

"You what!"

"I walked. It was about ten miles and singularly rough going."

"It's four, actually. But heavens, there was no need, man. I'd never have expected you to walk."

"I am not in the habit," said Mr. Hive with dignity, "of quitting a job just when it is becoming difficult."

"All right. What happened?"

"My report follows." Hive cleared his throat while he spread out before him a somewhat crumpled sheet of paper bearing penciled notes. When he spoke again, his normally pleasantly modulated voice had become measured and impersonal. The transformation sounded a bit of a strain.

"At approximately twenty-one thirty hours, I proceeded on foot to the premises at Hambourne Dyke, where the subject was understood to have arranged a rendezvous with Folkestone. I arrived at approximately twenty-two thirty hours and commenced observation. A car which I recognized as Folkestone's was standing in a concealed position at the side of the cottage. Investigation revealed no other vehicle—"

"Look, old chap, don't you think you could shorten all this a bit?"

Mr. Hive looked offended. He kept one finger marking the place he had reached while he explained that in matters such as this, one could not be too fastidious regarding the accuracy of evidence. He might add, with respect, that if anyone knew how a private detective's report ought to be framed, it was surely an experienced and conscientious private detective. . . .

"All right, all right. Get on, then. I'm sorry."

"Very well." Hive looked down again at his piece of paper. "No other vehicle . . . ah, yes." He straightened his shoulders. "I noticed signs that the premises were occupied. Lights were on in two of the rooms, one at the front

93

and one at the rear of the house. The curtains of both rooms were drawn. This made observation difficult, but in each case I was successful in obtaining a view of the interior through a gap in the aforementioned curtains.

"I established by this means that the room at the rear—which I confirmed as being a bedroom—had at that time no occupant. In the front room, however, I observed Folkestone. He was alone and appeared to be drinking. There was no sign of the subject, Calais. I kept Folkestone under observation until three o'clock. He left the room twice for short periods. The subject did not appear.

"At three o'clock I observed that Folkestone was asleep. I therefore took a short rest myself. . . ."

"Where?"

There was a pause. Mr. Hive was wondering whether a sound sleep in the parked car of a subject's lover came under the heading of reasonable expedients.

"I said, where?"

"I leaned against a tree. In this profession, one acquires a facility for going into a light doze on one's feet. I had, of course, set what I call my mental alarm clock to arouse me at a reasonable time."

"What time was that?"

"Half past six, actually. May I finish my report now?" Hive felt that some measure of his dignity was at stake. He would await an invitation to proceed. Several seconds went by. He remained obstinately silent.

"No," he heard at last, "there really wouldn't be any point. To be perfectly frank, the situation is not at all what it was."

"I am not sure that I understand."

"No, I'm sorry. The thing is, there has been a reconciliation."

"I am grieved to hear it," said Mr. Hive.

94

"You should not be. The saving of a marriage is matter for rejoicing, surely."

"I hope I have not failed to give satisfaction. I have taken a great deal of trouble, if you don't mind my mentioning it."

"Not at all. You have done splendidly."

"That is most kind of you. I do hope you understand, though, that in this field of work a single setback must not be regarded too pessimistically. Folkestone is not necessarily a broken reed, you know. If I might presume to advise a little more patience—"

"No, you might not. I wish nothing further done in the matter."

Mr. Hive sighed. "Just as you like." With his foot he eased the door of the booth open a couple of inches to freshen the hot, spent air.

"You may as well return to London at once. I think, in fact, that it would be advisable. Do you think you could prepare your account before you leave?"

Hive said he thought he might manage that.

"Good. Well, leave it in a sealed envelope with my name on it at that little shop near the station, the one I told you about. And whatever you do, don't mail it. Oh, incidentally . . ."

"Yes?"

"This isn't important in the least, but I just wondered if you'd happened to learn our friend Folkestone's real name."

"Oh, I . . ." Papers, a letter or two, an addressed packet idly glimpsed in pale morning light on the seat of the car at Hambourne Dyke . . . his nap in said car . . . better not say. "I never actually heard anybody call him anything."

95

"Doesn't matter. Doesn't matter at all. I couldn't care less now. Are you getting the car put right?"

"A garage is working on it."

"That's fine. Don't forget to put it on the bill. And thanks a lot for everything."

Hive thoughtfully replaced the receiver. So that was that. Odd bird. He came out of the booth and looked up at a blue sky dotted with harmless wisps of white. It was a perfect day for doing nothing in particular. Or—why not?— for paying a surprise call on an old friend. He smiled, and then remembered something and stopped smiling. His camera. He turned and stepped back into the telephone booth.

"Ah, Mr. Hive. I am so lad you thought to get in touch." What Mr. Clay really meant was that he was relieved that Hive was only on the telephone and not physically present in the school. "We have come across something here which I believe belongs to you."

"My purloined camera! Oh, joyful tidings!" Mr. Hive felt entitled, in the circumstances, to a little skittishness.

"Purloined, I cannot say," remarked the headmaster stiffly, "but camera it may well be. A large square leather case. I have recollection of your carrying something of the kind last night. . . ."

"I shall come at once."

"No, no," Mr. Clay said hastily. "I will not hear of it. It is now lunchtime. and boys are roaming, replete and unoccupied. Tasks are good for them. Where may you be found, Mr. Hive?"

"I can be at the Three Crowns in a very few minutes."

"Ye-e-ess . . . Perhaps a rendezvous *outside* the building—"

"As you wish."

"And, ah, if I might request that the boy be not given any opportunity to loiter—"

"Naturally."

By the time Hive reached the Three Crowns, a very small boy with glasses and a rumpled grammar school cap was standing outside the entrance to the public bar. The camera case was on the ground beside him. Mr. Hive hooked a penny from one of his waistcoat pockets and presented it to the boy with the air of conferring a golden guinea.

"Cut along, then, young shaver! You'll just have time to catch the tuck-shop before Latin!"

The boy stared as if at the sudden materialization of a character out of science fiction.

Mr. Hive picked up his case. "By the way, where did this turn up? Do you know?"

The boy went on staring a little longer. Then Hive's switch to intelligible English registered. The boy swallowed, sullenly mumbled, "Cupboard somewhere," and departed.

The next hour or so Mr. Hive spent very pleasantly in the devising of his account, inspired jointly by brandy and the now obvious approbation of the barmaid. Greeting him like an old friend, she had said that he might call her Helen and that she would call him Mort. She really was a splendid creature; he had not the heart to tell her that he would have preferred Mortimer ("Mort" sounded so unhappily like "wart").

"What's all that writing you're doing, Mort? Do tell me."

She was leaning forward across the bar, chin on hand, prettily amused by so much industry. Mr. Hive's table was only three feet away; there was no one else in the room, and he had moved it boldly out of line.

"I am preparing an account of professional fees and out-goings."

"You're not! You're writing a love letter!" She twisted her head a little, pretending to make out some of the words.

Hive smiled, not looking up. "Might I hope that you could be free for an hour or so this evening, Helen?"

"I daresay I could tell you—but only if you let me know what you're really writing."

"I've told you. I am making out an account."

"Honest?" Without taking her chin from her cupped hand, she delicately inserted into one nostril the tip of her little finger. "You a commercial traveler, then?"

Mr. Hive raised his head. "I am a private detective." He watched the girl's bantering manner fade. Her eyes widened, but she kept in them enough of disbelief to proclaim that she, Helen Banion, had not been born yesterday.

"I am not pulling your leg," added Mr. Hive with a touch of gravity that she allowed herself to find impressive. "The fact is that I undertook a certain commission that brought me to Flaxborough. My inquiries are complete. My client is satisfied." He spread his hands. "So now the bill."

"And a night off, by the sound of it."

"Exactly. At what time will you be free?"

"Well, I can't, actually. Not tonight." She looked thoughtfully at the finger end she had withdrawn from her nose, then nibbled it. "It's my day off tomorrow, though. If you're still here, I mean."

"Nothing," declared Mr. Hive warmly, "will be allowed to take me anywhere else!"

He drank and composed peacefully until closing time. The account, completed at last, was a copious document that ran to four pages of small writing. He decided it would do very nicely. There were lots of *to attending upon*s and *to making provision of*s, with here and there an *as per approved scale. Disbursements* abounded, and each and every charge was presented in multiples of a guinea. Mr. Justin Scorpe himself could scarcely have done better.

The man Purbright saw standing in the doorway of the lounge of Dunroamin was not quite as tall as himself. His hair, though crisp and glossily black still, had receded a good deal. The face was flushed and fleshy, the eyes quick-moving. He wore what the inspector took to be an expensive suit; it was just on the gray side of black, and it hung comfortably yet without spareness. The cloth had a soft-hard look, a sort of sleek durability. Under the open jacket, a white shirt—aggressively white—and narrow, tasteful tie—aggressively tasteful. The man's consciously erect bearing and his mannerism of occasionally thrusting back his shoulders could not quite disguise the buildup of fat that paunched over the trouser band and breastily plumped the shirt.

"Mr. Palgrove . . ." Purbright rose from the chair in which he had been sitting and moved not toward the door but rather aside from it; he did not want to seem to be inviting the man into his own room. Palgrove nodded to him, then to Love, and slowly came farther in.

"I'm afraid this is rather a sad homecoming for you, sir."

Again Palgrove nodded, his face blank. He looked about him at the floor, at the chairs, then sat in one, well forward with his hands on his knees. He had not forgotten to give his trousers a high, crease-preserving hitch.

Purbright resumed his own seat so that Palgrove should not feel that he was being questioned from a perhaps intimidating angle.

"You've heard from the officer what has happened, I suppose, sir?"

"The gist of it, yes. No details."

The voice came to Purbright as something of a surprise. It was not exactly brisk, yet its slightly Cockney curtness was in unexpected contrast to Palgrove's expression of weary abstraction. The inspector reminded himself that the effects of emotional stress were never predictable; a board room tone was probably part of a determination not to break down.

"We are by no means sure yet how the accident happened, Mr. Palgrove. It is not so much a question of how your wife came to slip into the water as why she was unable to extricate herself."

"Poor old Henny was daft about those damned goldfish." Again a staccato, matter-of-fact announcement.

"Was Mrs. Palgrove in fairly normal health?"

"Nothing wrong so far as I know. Nothing serious."

"I was thinking of heart trouble, Mr. Palgrove. Or of anything that might have made her subject to blackouts."

A slow headshake. "You think she could have passed out?"

"It does seem the only explanation. Who was her doctor?"

Palgrove thought for a moment. "Used to be old Hillyard. But that was a while back."

"Doctor Hillyard has not been in practice for some years," Purbright said. Out of the corner of his eye, he glimpsed Love's smirk; it was in fact exactly ten years since the conviction and imprisonment of that luckless practitioner.

"No, I'm sorry; can't tell you."

"Never mind, sir. Now, about these goldfish—was it usual for Mrs. Palgrove to go out and feed them at night?"

"Don't know about feeding. She'd go and look at them

100

at the oddest times. Show them off to anybody who called."

"Do you happen to know if she was expecting a visitor last night?"

"No idea. Wouldn't be surprised, though. She was on committees and things, you know. Those people are always in and out of each other's houses."

Palgrove had begun to glance around nervously. He stood. "Look, can I get you fellows a drink? Whiskey?"

Love, who thought that all liquor other than ginger wine tasted rather awful, declined. Purbright accepted.

He watched Palgrove let down the door of a cocktail cabinet. A light went on inside it, setting glasses and bottles aglitter and frosting the outlines of birds engraved on the compartment's mirror backing. At the same time, a mechanical tinkling started to form itself into a tune.

Palgrove, unscrewing the whiskey bottle, glanced to see Love's round stare of admiration. "Hundred and eighty quid, this little number," he said.

When drinks had been poured, Palgrove handed one to the inspector and carried his own to the fireplace, where he remained standing. He took several sips of the whiskey, licked his mouth carefully—appreciatively, too, Purbright thought—and set the glass on the mantelpiece beside one of a pair of china storks that must have been nearly two feet high. Then he said: "The funeral—I've been wondering about the funeral. You know—"

"You can go ahead with the preliminary arrangements. Sergeant Malley will be in touch with you about the inquest. You'll find him very helpful."

"Inquest—that's necessary, is it?"

"I'm afraid so, sir. Unless, of course, it turns out that your wife's doctor was seeing her regularly and confirms the postmortem findings. Then he'll issue his certificate, I've no doubt."

Palgrove remained silent. During the pause, Purbright did some mental molding on his next question.

"There is one possibility that the coroner is always required to examine when anything like this happens. I suppose you realize what that is, sir? Oh, a very remote possibility, certainly, but it has to be disposed of."

Palgrove's incredulous stare wavered after the first few seconds, as if it might turn to laughter. "Good God, man, who'd want to murder poor old Henny?"

The inspector frowned. "I wasn't thinking of murder, sir."

"Sorry. My mistake."

"The question I had in mind was whether your wife could have done what she did otherwise than by accident. You must know her personality, her state of mind, if she was worried about anything. . . . Any eccentricities of behavior, for instance."

"I don't know. I'd have to think about that."

"Yes, do, sir."

Purbright leaned back a couple of inches and gazed blandly at his tumbler. He tipped it gently to one side, then the other, and watched the fine oily rivulets of spirit creep down the glass.

"It's funny, you know," Palgrove said at last, "but I shouldn't be surprised if there was something in what you say."

"Oh, I didn't mean you to—"

Palgrove held up his hand. "No, I know you didn't. Facts are facts, though. And I can't pretend that Henny's attitude to things was altogether normal. She had these terrific enthusiasms, you know. It seemed sometimes that animals meant more to her than human beings. It was her kindness, really, I suppose. I mean, I wouldn't knock her for that.

Not now. But she got so worked up about these things. Perhaps I should have seen that there was a danger of her—you know—sort of going over the top."

"Did Mrs. Palgrove do much letter writing, sir?"

"Lord, you can say that again. You certainly can. She was forever writing letters. Mind you, she was on committees galore."

"So I understand. I wasn't thinking so much of formal correspondence, though. Have you ever known her to write a—what shall I say—an excitable sort of letter?"

"To be quite honest, I never took that much interest. She'd be capable of it, though. I'm sure she would. She was an excitable sort of woman." Palgrove paused to eye the inspector carefully. "Why, has something of that kind—?"

"It was a hypothetical question, sir. I'm just trying to get a general idea of your wife's temperament."

Palgrove looked at his glass, empty now. He stretched and flexed his shoulders. "Can I get you another drink, Inspector?"

"No, thank you, sir. We'll have to be getting back."

Palgrove went to pour a second whiskey for himself. He spoke over his shoulder. "This inquest thing—"

"Yes, sir?"

"I suppose I ought to get my solicitor on the job."

"That's a matter for you to decide, Mr. Palgrove. He would accompany you if you wished, I'm sure."

"I'll have to think about it." He drank his whiskey at one steady tilt, then smacked his lips. He stood the glass on the top of the cabinet, paused, picked it up again and walked with it in his hand to the door, where the two policemen were already waiting. He smiled wryly at them, showed them the glass. "My own washer-up from now on, I suppose."

Seated in the Widow on its sedate return run to the police station, Love said to the inspector: "What do you make of Pally, then?"

"What do you think I should make of him?"

"I reckon he's a bit of a rum bugger."

"You could be right."

"They say he's fooling around with some tottie from Jubilee Park way."

"That's one thing I admire about you, Sid. You have an eye for geographical detail."

"You don't really believe his wife did herself in, do you?"

"No, I don't. But it was very interesting to see how appealing a theory Mr. Palgrove found it, once it was suggested."

9

THE offices of the Flaxborough and Eastern Counties Charities Alliance were on the first floor of what once had been the town house of a Georgian wine merchant. They were reached by narrow stairs from a door between a drugstore and a hardware store. The door was surmounted by a semicircular fanlight and flanked by narrow fluted pillars; traces of its original moldings were just discernible as depressions and swellings in the buildup of countless layers of paint.

Mr. Hive sniffed as he climbed the steep, uneven stairs. The smell of kerosene from the hardware store contended with whiffs of cosmetics and cough syrup from the drugstore. Near the top, though, another, more pungent, aroma asserted itself. Hive paused to savor it. He smiled.

He arrived at a broad landing flooded with light from a ten-feet-high window. There were three doors. On one of them he read: F.E.C.C.A.—Secretary and Accounts. He knocked, then softly pushed it open a few inches, enough to introduce one cautious, reconnoitering eye. This he withdrew after a moment or two.

"I said, come in." A woman's voice, querulous, refined.

Hive reached something from his pocket—a small, squat bottle—and remaining himself out of sight, dangled it between finger and thumb just inside the room.

Miss Lucilla Edith Cavell Teatime pushed her basket chair back from the table and half rose, staring at the quarter-pint-sized apparition that had floated through the door. She read its label. Highland Fling. Resolutely Miss Teatime walked to the door and pulled it fully open.

"Mortimer!"

"Lucy!"

The bottle of whiskey hung disregarded on the periphery of their embrace. Then, stepping back, Mr. Hive presented it to Miss Teatime with a deep bow.

She stood regarding him fondly. "How sweet of you, Mortimer, to remember my little twinges."

"Nonsense. Any doctor would have done the same."

She laughed, as if at a distant memory. "Poor Mortimer, that did not last very long, did it?"

"A fill gap. Not one of my best ideas."

"You are intrinsically too honest, my dear. That bravura of yours was bound to let you down."

"You said so, Lucy. You said so at the time."

"I think your present occupation suits you much better."

He raised his brows. "You know what it is, then?"

"But of course. Kitty keeps in touch with me, you know. And Uncle Macnamara."

She turned and walked to a small cupboard set in the wall. "I do hope you do not object to drinking from a teacup." She arranged cups and saucers on a tray, together with a sugar basin and a milk jug. The china was white, patterned delicately with tiny clusters of forget-me-nots. Miss Teatime sluiced a substantial slug of Highland Fling into each cup.

Mr. Hive sat down at the table. Miss Teatime pushed a

pile of papers aside to make room for his cup and saucer. He sighed happily. "How nice it is to see you again."

"Are you here for long? I suppose I cannot prevail upon you to follow my example and leave London. This altogether charming town has been a revelation to me."

"It certainly has its attractions," conceded Mr. Hive, barmaidenly blushes in mind.

"I fancy I should find town somewhat dull now. Londoners are so parochial. Anyway, they spend most of their lives sealed up in little containers of one kind or another."

Hive glanced around the bright, spacious room. The paneled walls had been painted a pale dove gray. In the center of one was an oil painting of a great fenland church with sheep huddled in complacent possession of the graveyard. Upon another hung four framed colored prints depicting, Hive supposed, specimen candidates for compassion: a pinafored child asleep on the steps of a public house, an emaciated greyhound, two sorrowful donkeys being belabored by a man with a black beard and leggings, and a puppy cornered by three villainous-looking surgeons holding an assortment of cutlery behind their backs.

"You're making out all right, then, Lucy, are you?"

"I am being kept nicely occupied, and that is the main thing. You can have no idea, Mortimer, of how much room there is in the charities field for proper organization. I confess I have found the work quite exciting."

"It's not the sort of thing I would have thought easy to corner."

"There is unfortunately a long tradition of rivalry between the various endeavors. The animal factions are especially difficult to reconcile, but once they see the wastefulness of dissipated effort, I am sure the situation can be— what is the modern jargon?—rationalized."

Miss Teatime reached for her handbag, opened it, and

produced a brown cardboard pack. "May I tempt you?"

Hive slapped his knee. "I knew it! I knew I was right! I could smell those damn things from halfway down the stairs. D'you remember what the Cullen boys used to call them in the old days at Frascati's?"

Miss Teatime smiled dreamily as she put a match to the slim black cheroot. "Tadger Cullen . . . dear me, yes . . . and little Arnold . . ."

"Lucy's gelding sticks, Tadger used to call them. Remember, he had that weird theory about cigars and sterility."

"The Cullens could be a little embarrassing on occasion, but I do not think they meant any real harm." She regarded the tip of her cheroot awhile, then looked up perkily. "Guess with whom I have been in correspondence during the past few days?"

Hive shook his head.

"Your old friend Mr. Holbein."

"Fruity Holbein? Don't tell me, you're going to bring one-armed bandits into the good cause."

"Indeed, no. Let me explain. It happens that I am blessed with a very progressive committee. I have convinced its members that the efficiency of the organization would be increased enormously by the installation of a computer—"

"Good God!"

"To say nothing of the prestige such a contrivance would bestow upon them personally. They were very pleased indeed to learn that a computer of modest capacity could be purchased through a friend of mine in the trade for as little as two hundred and fifty pounds. The sum has now been allocated, and Mr. Holbein has set to work."

"What on earth does Fruity know about computers?"

"He has assured me," said Miss Teatime, "that he can produce a very persuasive article. I am not myself mechanically minded, but he did tell me that it was a simple matter of something called pinball cannibalization.

"But there"—she uncorked the bottle and replenished their teacups—"we have talked sufficiently about my little interests. Now you must tell me of yourself. How goes"—her voice dropped significantly—"the *case?*"

"Oh, it's over," said Mr. Hive breezily. "All but the fellow paying the bill, anyway."

"A successful termination, of course?"

"By no means—although I don't blame myself. The parties are reconciled."

"Oh, what a waste of your time, Mortimer. I hope they are thoroughly ashamed of themselves."

"I doubt it. One thing I've learned—the private eye gets precious little consideration in this country. He's been given what they nowadays call a bad image."

"Public ignorance, Mortimer, public ignorance. What can you expect"—Miss Teatime gazed sternly out of the window—"of a generation brought up to think that life is all cock and candyfloss?"

Over the telephone to Purbright came the impatient, matter-of-fact voice of Doctor Fergusson.

"This woman from what-d'you-call-it, Brompton Gardens . . ."

"Oh, yes, Doctor?"

"I thought I'd better give you a call. Something a bit odd. It'll be in the report, of course, but it might be as well for you to know straightaway."

"I see."

"She did drown. No doubt about that. No evidence of organic disease—nothing significant, anyway. Time of death —hang on a minute . . . yes, eleven last night, give or

109

take a bit—before midnight, certainly, but not more than an hour or an hour and a half before. . . ."

"Between ten thirty and twelve, then?"

"That's what I said. Yes. Now, then, here's the queer thing. Are you listening?"

"Yes."

"Right. Well, there's quite definite bruising on both ankles. A set, a distinct set of five bruises on each. Just at the bottom of the lower leg. And both sets match."

"Fingers?"

"I'd say there's not a doubt of it."

The inspector waited a moment, but Fergusson did not elaborate.

"Any other marks, Doctor?"

"Well, I didn't intend to give you the full report over the phone, you know."

"Naturally not. I do appreciate your having told me this much. It was just that I wondered if the body showed signs of injury."

"Bruises are injuries, old man. No, it's all right, I see what you mean. There were other marks, actually. Knuckles, elbows—abrasions, you know. If what we're both thinking is true, she must have flayed about a bit, poor soul. And there was a broad bruise just over the diaphragm."

"Where she hit the wall when she was pushed over . . ."

"Speculation's your job, not mine. I don't think I'd argue on that one, though. Not really."

Click. Fergusson had quit the line.

Purbright took his tidings to the office of the chief constable. Mr. Chubb, gravely nibbling the last of the three whole-wheat biscuits that came with his afternoon pot of tea, heard him out in silence. Then, as Purbright had known he would, he shook his head slowly and said: "It sounds an unpleasant business, Mr. Purbright."

"I'm afraid it does, sir."

"Mind you, I must say it's very hard to credit. She's done some splendid work, you know, this woman. My wife knows her well. They were on several committees together. She'll be upset about this."

"She was popular, was she—Mrs. Palgrove?"

"Oh, I don't know about popular, exactly. All these good ladies squabble a bit at times, you know. I've heard she was inclined to rule the roost. But good gracious, that's no reason why anyone should . . . Brompton Gardens . . . No, I can't understand it at all."

"You remember that letter you received, sir? The unsigned one."

"Letter?" Mr. Chubb looked politely bemused.

"Yes, sir. The one beginning 'My Dear Friend' and making some rather dramatic allegations—"

"Ah, that one—well, of course, it came to me in error, didn't it? If you remember, Mr. Purbright, you sent a man over especially to collect it."

"You recall its terms, though?"

"Vaguely. Are you suggesting it might have some relevance? Whoever it was meant for, it did seem a rather wild letter."

"I think it *was* meant for you, sir, and I think that we shall find that Mrs. Palgrove wrote it."

Mr. Chubb counted his fingernails. Satisfied that they were all there, he said: "I suppose you'll be wanting to cast around to see if any of the neighbors noticed what was going on last night."

"I was going to propose that Pooke and Broadleigh start on that straightaway, sir. I shall go back to the house. The husband will be either there or within call, I imagine. Perhaps a search warrant, sir, just in case?"

Mr. Chubb nodded gloomily.

Purbright went on. "I shouldn't imagine this has anything to do with Mrs. Palgrove's death, but there has been a rather curious feud lately among the organizers of some of the local charities. They've been busy sabotaging one another's efforts—or that's what it looks like. As you know, Mrs. Palgrove was a good deal involved in charity work. We shall have to satisfy ourselves that personal antagonism on somebody's part did not sharpen into actual violence."

The chief constable was quite shrewd enough to divine behind Purbright's careful form of words a distinct eagerness to see this bizarre theory confirmed by events. In such a mood, the inspector tended to make him nervous.

"You must do as you think fit, Mr. Purbright," he said coolly.

Purbright remained at headquarters only long enough to acquaint Sergeant Malley with the new situation and to brief detectives Pooke and Broadleigh. Then, accompanied by Love, he drove to Brompton Gardens.

The uniformed man, Fairclough, had been rejoined by Harper, and both were leaning disconsolately against the posts of the well, looking from a distance a little like the lion and the unicorn on the royal coat of arms.

Fairclough said that Palgrove had left an hour or so previously for his office. Purbright sent him into the house to telephone a request for Palgrove's return. "Tell him you understand it's fairly urgent—just fairly, mind; don't frighten the poor man."

To Harper, he explained a different errand. "I want this thing completely drained. You'd better go down personally to Fire Service headquarters and see Budge. One of their small pumps should be adequate. How many gallons would you say there are in that thing?"

Harper pursed his lips and scowled. He hadn't the faintest idea.

"Twenty cubic feet?" Purbright suggested helpfully.

Harper maintained his scowl of pretended calculation. "Mmm . . . nearer twenty-one."

"Good man," said the inspector. "Oh, and you'd better mention the fish. Budge might want to bring nets or jars or something."

He and Love walked toward the house. Fairclough, on his way back from telephoning, paused in the doorway. "Don't shut it," Purbright called.

"It's all right, sir; Mr. Palgrove left us a key."

"Very civil of him. Did you get through?"

"He's coming at once, sir."

In the lounge, Purbright walked directly to the writing cabinet he had noticed earlier. It was open. He sat before it, took a sheet of plain gray correspondence paper from a dozen or so lying beside a stack of the overprinted Four Foot Haven paper, and wound it into the typewriter. He typed: *Dear Friend, This is an urgent appeal. I am in great danger.* He withdrew the sheet and unfolded one of exactly the same size and color and texture that he had taken from his pocket.

"Now, then, Sid, let's see what we've got."

Love stood by Purbright's shoulder as letter by letter, the inspector compared the typing sample he had made with the opening lines of one of the three mailed appeals. The sergeant watched a pencil point hover over identically blocked *e*'s, then move from one to another of the *p*'s with slightly deformed stems. Every *n* was out of alignment to the same degree; every full stop had been rendered oversize by a similar amount of wear.

"She did write those letters, then," Love said.

"I don't think there can be much doubt of it."

"So she must have guessed what was going to happen to her."

"It looks rather like it."

Love leaned lower and read the whole letter through. He pointed to the sentence: *"The person whose loyal and faithful companion I have been—and to whom even now my life is dedicated—intends to have me done away with."*

"That's a pretty obvious hint."

"Rather more than a hint, Sid. It's practically straight identification."

"Of Palgrove, of course?"

"Well, who else?"

"A lover?" suggested Love hopefully.

"Whose loyal and faithful companion I have been . . . no, I don't feel that's the sort of phrase one would use in relation to an affair. It's wife language, I should have thought."

Love's finger moved down the page. "Look at this—*perhaps to be held helpless underwater by a loved hand until I drown . . .* Nasty bit of prophecy that turned out to be."

"I wonder," Purbright said, "whom she meant by 'they.' You see—*They think I do not understand.* And here—*I have heard the plan discussed . . .*"

"The husband and a girl friend?"

"The inference is invited, certainly."

"She could have been snooping on them."

"It's more likely that he was careless over some telephone conversation. As you probably noticed, he has a very penetrating voice."

"Are you going to tackle him about the letter?"

"It will have to be put to him sooner or later."

"And the girl friend? If there is one."

"Ah, now that's a question that must be pursued straightaway. And very diligently."

Love seemed to have run out of observations. Humming

114

quietly to himself, he wandered around the room. He paused by the cocktail cabinet, tempted to set it playing its tinkly music again. Better not. He examined the opulently tubed television set, fashioned in mock Jacobean. Over to the window. Nice curtains. Very nice. If he had a house like this, he'd not want to spoil everything by murdering somebody. Whatever got into people to . . .

"What I cannot for the life of me understand," said Purbright, "is what good she thought this letter was going to do her. She didn't even sign it, and she obviously changed her mind about enclosing a photograph."

"Yes, but doesn't it say something about writing again?"

"True. *Soon I shall send you details of how you can help.* A coroner. A chief constable. A newspaper editor. Why those three? Why not just the chief constable? He seems the most appropriate, in the circumstances."

"We don't know that she didn't send letters to other people," Love said. "Maybe they just threw them away. I should."

Purbright turned and regarded him sternly. "A fine confession from a detective sergeant."

"Well, you must admit she sounds nutty."

"Oh, I do," said Purbright. He swung around again and began leafing through some letters and copies of letters that he had found. Love settled himself into an armchair and gazed dreamily out of the window. Five minutes went by.

"Hello," the inspector said suddenly, "here's an old friend." He separated a sheet of paper from the rest and leaned back to study it. "Remember Miss Teatime, Sid?"

"What, the old girl from London?"

"Don't make her sound decrepit; she's fifty-two, actually, I believe. And very well preserved."

115

Love pouted dubiously but did not argue. The inspector, he happened to know, was fifty-one. "What's she been up to now?"

"Sabotaging a dog shelter, if we are to believe Mrs. Palgrove. Mrs. P seems to have sent her one of those if-the-shoe-fits letters."

"She's pretty hot on letter writing. Was, rather."

"How long has Miss Teatime been concerned with good works, Sid?"

"No idea. All I heard was that she'd taken some sort of secretarial job in St. Anne's Gate. They reckon she has private means."

"It's a very sharp letter," Purbright said, thoughtfully. "Listen . . . *It may interest you to know that certain information has reached me privately concerning the disposal of funds raised not a hundred miles from here in the name of so-called charity. I am reluctant to pass this information to the authorities, but I shall not hesitate to do so if the need arises.*"

"You did mention," said Love after a pause, "that Miss Teatime is well preserved. . . ."

"Oh, come, Sid, you mustn't jump too far ahead. Anyway"—he looked at the date on the letter—"this was only written yesterday. It wouldn't have reached the lady until this morning—always assuming that it was mailed at all."

Love listened, but not very attentively. He pursued his theme. "She was more than a match for that chap over at Benstone, remember."

They heard the thrum of an approaching sports car.

"Pally's back, by the sound of it," said Love.

10

THE news of Henrietta Palgrove's untimely end had coursed by midday to the farthest tendrils of the Flaxborough social grapevine. And within three hours of Doctor Fergusson's laying down his scalpel and trotting fussily to the telephone, there had followed along those same mysteriously efficient channels the assertion that she had died of a felonious upending.

Not everyone believed it. Such stories had gone the rounds before and had proved to be the sanguine embroideries of a succession of citizens devoted to the dogma of No Smoke without Fire. Skepticism was greatest in the immediate neighborhood of Dunroamin. The Palgroves' fellow residents were not to be deceived by the arrival of the police, an ambulance, or even a detachment of firemen. They recognized in this latest rumor yet another malicious attempt to depress property values in the area and were ready to combat it.

It was only to be expected, then, that detectives Pooke and Broadleigh should find not a single householder in Brompton Gardens who could recall anything heard or seen during the past twenty-four hours that might have a bearing on what they all persisted in calling "poor Mrs. Palgrove's accident."

Nor was anyone unwary enough to admit knowledge of any aspect of the Palgroves' private life that did not reflect credit on both partners. They were comfortably off. They were quiet. One or both went, it was thought, to church. Their lawns were kept mown. What more could be desired of neighbors?

"We're just wasting our time; you know that, don't you?" Broadleigh said at last to Pooke as he closed behind them the gate of Red Gables.

Pooke said he did know; he'd had experience of this lot before.

"It's the tradesmen we ought to be talking to," said Broadleigh. "Especially the ones who haven't been paid for a bit. They're the boys for information."

"Not half," Pooke said.

They crossed the road and sauntered slowly toward their final call, the house next door to Dunroamin.

A boy with a deep canvas bag of newspapers slung from one shoulder emerged from a drive farther back. He hurried after the two men, staring fixedly at their backs. He reached them just as Pooke was stooping to open a gate.

"You policemen?" the boy asked, not disrespectfully.

They viewed him carefully up and down, keeping their distance. Then, having decided apparently that he was neither wired nor fused, they nodded to signify that he might speak again.

The boy did so. "You asking questions about that lady that got drowneded?" He jerked his head. "Next door?"

"We might be," said Broadleigh, limbering up his jaw muscles a little.

From Pooke: "Why? What can you tell us about it, son?" He made his voice friendly.

The boy swallowed and gave his bag a hitch. "Just that they were having a row last night."

"Who?"

"Her and her old man."

"Quarreling, you mean?"

"Going on at each other. You know—shouting and that."

Broadleigh beckoned the boy into the shelter of the drive. All three stood under the trailing branches of a laburnum. A notebook appeared. "Now, then, son—what's your name?"

In the grounds of Dunroamin a pump throbbed. Two firemen wearing shiny black thigh boots stood looking at the rapidly descending surface of the water in the well. One held a stick with a wire mesh hemisphere at its end. Now and again he made a sudden lunge with the stick and brought up glittering in the basket a threshing orange fish, which he tipped into a small cistern.

The other fireman held out his hand. "Let's have a go."

"Only one left. Crafty bugger, an' all."

After some ineffectual scooping, the survivor was captured. A minute later the last of the water disappeared with a noise like German political oratory.

Hearing the sharp rise in the tone of the pump, Harper and Fairclough came out of the house, where they had been having a cup of tea in the kitchen, and joined the firemen.

Harper peered down at the weedy mud in the well's bottom.

"That'll be a nice job."

Rubbing his hands down his trouser seams as if in anticipation, he looked about him and then wandered across to a small wooden shed. When he came back, he was carrying a rake.

Inspector Purbright also had heard the pump motor

change its note. There hadn't been much water in that thing after all, he thought. Enough, though. He looked at Palgrove's hands while he was speaking. They were podgy, but large; the long thumbs, their ends back-curved, seemed especially powerful. From the wrists black hair sprouted.

"You'll appreciate what a difference has been made by this report of the doctor's, Mr. Palgrove. I've been perfectly frank about it because I want to know if you can suggest an explanation of the bruises on your wife's legs—an explanation, that is, other than the sinister but obvious one."

"Hundreds of things can cause bruising."

"Symmetrical bruises? Five each side? And spaced so?" Purbright held his hands in a posture of grasping two upright poles.

"Yes, but you don't *know*. I mean, nobody can say for certain, just looking at marks."

"I'm sorry, sir, but I think you can take it from me that these particular marks can be interpreted in only one way."

The sound of Love's turning over a page of the notebook in which he was clawing down shorthand on the other side of the room drew a glance from Palgrove. He looked not nervous but hurt and perplexed.

"Does he *have* to?" Palgrove murmured to the inspector.

"I'm afraid he does, sir," Purbright said.

Palgrove reached to his inside breast pocket, paused, then patted both side pockets. From one he drew a pack of cigarettes. He offered it to Purbright and bleakly noted his shake of the head. He lit a cigarette himself. The pack he laid on his chair arm.

"I should like you to tell me now," Purbright said, "everything you did last night. From teatime, say, until you arrived at your office this morning. Take you time, sir; I'd prefer you to be fairly precise."

Palgrove stared at the opposite wall, then at his cigarette, which he held in the bottom of the cleft between his second and third fingers.

"This is going to sound a bit unlikely," he said. "What I mean to say is, if it's alibis you're thinking about, I suppose I just haven't got one."

"You mustn't worry about what you suppose I'm wanting you to say, Mr. Palgrove. So long as it's true, what I'm able to make of it is my problem."

"Yes. Well . . ." Palgrove took time off to draw on the cigarette, sweep his hand clear, and expel smoke upward with noisy determination. He picked a shred of tobacco from his upper lip; his tongue tip continued to explore the spot.

"I had made arrangements to go to Leicester, actually. Seeing about some machinery."

"Yes, sir?"

"I was hoping to stay over with an old friend of mine. Wilcox, he's called. On the board of Hardy-Livingstone. Anyway, I left here round about six."

"By car?"

"In the A.M., yes."

Purbright frowned. "I thought we were talking about the evening, sir."

"That's right . . . Oh, I get you. No. A.M.—Aston Martin."

"I see."

"As I was saying, I left here about six. I'd had a spot to eat with the wife—not much, I'm not a tea man—and told her where I was going, of course, and that I'd be back some time in the morning."

"Would you say it was usual or unusual for you to spend a night away from home?"

"I don't know—unusual, I suppose, really. But I have

121

to, occasionally. Henny didn't mind. She'd lots of interests of her own." He took another fierce suck at his cigarette and leaned back to blow at the ceiling. "Anyway, to cut a long story short, there was I, halfway to Leicester, when I thought I heard one of the tappets knocking. Well, I was a bit put out because the car had only just been in for a service yesterday, and Henderson's generally pretty efficient. So what I did was to pull off to the side and have a proper listen under the lid. I couldn't trace a damn thing wrong. I went on a few more miles, and damn me if it didn't start again. Same old pantomime—pull off, listen, fiddle around —nothing. Three times I did that. In the end I just tried to forget about it and bashed on. But naturally I'd lost a lot of time. I didn't get to Leicester until . . . oh, must have been nine at least. I was a bit tired—you know, fed up— and there didn't seem much point in chasing up the fellow I'd come to see. Anyway—"

"Excuse me, sir, but wouldn't eight or even seven o'clock in the evening be a rather unconventional time to discuss business in any case?"

"I suppose you could say that, yes. But I just don't happen to be conventional. It doesn't pay, Inspector. Not these days."

"All right, sir. Go on."

"Well, to cut a long story short, I drove around to Tony Wilcox's place and saw straightaway that I'd boobed. Not a light in the place. I thought, should I wait? Then—no, I thought, they might not be back for hours, and it would hardly be on for me to be waiting for them on the doorstep, the uninvited guest. Not at that time of night. So I just turned around and started back."

"To Flaxborough?"

"Sure. Now then, I don't know whether you know a pub

called the Feathers, just the other side of Melton Mowbray—"

There was a knock on the door. Love went over and opened it. Palgrove glimpsed a man in uniform. The man murmured something to Love, who turned and gave Purbright a questioning look. "It's Fairclough, sir—if you could just spare a minute."

The inspector spared three. When he came back into the room, he apologized to Palgrove and invited him to continue.

"Yes. This pub. It wasn't the Feathers, actually—I must have been mixing it up with another one. I don't know its name, but it's somewhere yon side of Melton. The point is that I stopped there for a drink. It was nice and comfortable, so I had another one. I was tired, and of course I'd had nothing to eat. Anyway, to cut a long story short, I'd drunk four or maybe five whiskies by the time I left. And as soon as I started to drive again, I knew I was going to feel woozy. So I did the sensible thing and pulled off the road there and then. I went bang off to sleep and didn't wake up until nine o'clock this morning."

There was a long pause. Then Palgrove shrugged. "Sounds silly, but there you are." He looked toward the cocktail cabinet. Love hoped he would let it give another performance, but Palgrove remained seated.

Purbright spoke, "When you left your wife yesterday evening, she was quite normal, was she? In good health, I mean. Not upset in any way."

"Oh, yes. Perfectly."

"Was she expecting a visitor, do you know?"

"I don't think so. No one in particular. I told you, though, various people did call. People mixed up with this social work of hers."

"It would be helpful if you could tell us who these people were, sir."

Palgrove looked dubious. "Well, I'll try, but I didn't take all that interest, actually. Some of them I know. Mrs. Arnold, from up the road. She's one of the dog ones. Then the woman from that Red Cross place—Miss Ironside. Oh, and a schoolteacher called . . . no, wait a minute, he's not—he's something to do with insurance, I think. Can't remember his name. Then the vicar, of course—Mr. Haines. I've seen a couple of others occasionally, but I've no idea who they are."

The inspector waited. "No one else you can think of, sir?"

"No. I mean, they weren't people I had anything to do with myself."

Palgrove stretched restlessly. Again his hand went to the breast pocket inside his jacket. Purbright watched. He smiled, leaned forward.

"Is this what you are looking for, sir?"

Surprise lightening his face, Palgrove took the slim, yellow metal case. "Hello, where did that turn up?"

Purbright looked pleasant, said nothing.

"Well, thanks, anyway," Palgrove said. He turned the case about in his hand. "It's only plated, actually. Eighteen quid, all the same." Slickly he opened it.

"What the hell . . ."

Purbright looked with polite interest at the five brown, sodden cigarettes. "Hasn't done them much good, has it?"

Hostility was in Palgrove's eye. He stared at the policeman. "I don't get it."

"That is your case, sir?"

"Of course it is."

"The officers found it a short while ago at the bottom

124

of your garden well, Mr. Palgrove. Where your wife was drowned."

"Hey, now hold on a minute . . ."

"Yes, sir?"

Palgrove's anger rose. "Now look, I can see what you're bloody well getting at. But you're quite wrong. How the hell could I have had anything to do with—with what happened to Henny when I wasn't anywhere near the place? I know nothing about it at all. Absolutely nothing."

"Can you suggest how that case came to be in the water, sir?"

"Of course I can't."

"When was it last in your possession?"

"Yesterday, I should think. Yes, I had it at teatime. I must have left it around in this room somewhere."

"Did your wife smoke?"

"No."

"So it's not likely that she had the case with her when she went out to the well?"

"You don't know that. She could easily have picked it up. I mean, she was always tidying things up. For that matter, she could have chucked it into the water herself. I wouldn't put it past her."

Purbright considered. "That does rather sound as if you and Mrs. Palgrove did not always get on very well. I hadn't realized. I'm sorry."

"Good heavens, all married couples disagree occasionally."

"True, sir, but they don't all throw away valuable cigarette cases to spite one another."

"Now, look, Inspector—if you think you can goad me into—"

Purbright's hand went up. "Perish the thought, Mr. Palgrove."

"Yes, well don't be so damned provocative." He was silent a moment. "I'm sorry, but this has been one hell of a shock. I suppose I'm a bit on edge. No, the fact is that Henny and I got along as well as most. Not around each other's necks all the time, but so what? I certainly wouldn't have done her any harm."

"Mr. Palgrove, was your wife a wildly imaginative woman?"

"I wouldn't have said so. She was a bit gone on animals. . . . But look, we went into all that when you were here before."

"That's right, we did. But if I might say so, you are not in quite the same mood as you were then. That is perfectly natural. First reaction to shock can often take a form that people might mistake for flippancy."

"Did you think I was being flippant?"

"No, sir. I think *brittle* would be a better word. My impression is that you are now more inclined to consider the seriousness of your own position. For instance, you said at our first interview that your wife got so worked up about some things that she was in danger of going 'over the top,' as you put it. You spoke of her abnormality of attitude, her excitability, her passion for letter writing. But now you are taking some pains to present Mrs. Palgrove as a fairly ordinary housewife with ordinary enthusiasms and lapses of temper. Is this because you have realized that your earlier picture was certain to be contradicted by other people?"

"I've not thought about what other people might say. Why should I? I've not done anything."

Purbright leaned forward and picked up the gold-plated case from the chair arm, where Palgrove had placed it beside his packet of cigarettes. "I shan't deprive you of this longer than necessary, sir. The sergeant will give you a receipt." He nodded to Love.

126

Palgrove watched with sullen resignation. He saw the inspector take a sheet of paper from his pocket, unfold it and hold it toward him.

"I'd like you to look at that letter, if you will, sir. Then perhaps we can talk about it."

Slowly and with a deepening scowl, Palgrove read the letter through.

He shook his head. "What am I supposed to make of this?"

"We believe that it was written by your wife."

"Why should you? It's not even signed."

"Whose typewriter is that over there, sir?"

"My wife's."

"Well, it was certainly typed on that machine. It seems reasonable to assume that it was she who typed it."

"All right. You tell me what it means. It's a string of rubbish as far as I'm concerned. Just rubbish." Palgrove slid the letter dismissively into Purbright's lap and picked up his cigarettes.

"Oh, come, sir. The implication is plain enough. I'm not saying that I believe it or disbelieve it. But you mustn't pretend that you can't understand what she's getting at."

"It's bloody rubbish, man. I'm not going to waste time discussing it." Anger, bewilderment, fright all stood in Palgrove's blood-suffused face. He hid it behind the hand-cupped lighting of a cigarette.

"Very well, sir." Purbright carefully refolded the letter and put it, together with Palgrove's case, into a large buff envelope. He stood.

"There's just one other little matter I'd like to clear up. If you wouldn't mind coming out with me to your car."

Palgrove, hunched with ill grace, stumped doorward. Purbright followed him out, tweaking Love into tow.

The Aston Martin, splendidly agleam, stood on the drive

127

near the side door. For a moment, possessive pride modified Palgrove's air of exasperation. He stepped to one side and watched the inspector's face.

Purbright opened the car door and slued himself carefully into the driving seat. He glanced about him. Palgrove drew close and leaned on the door pillar.

"I'm looking," Purbright said, "for your service-record chart. You do keep something of that kind, sir?"

"Over there. Compartment on the left."

Palgrove gazed gloomily at the inspector's questing hand. He watched him open a folder, put a finger against an entry, peer at the instrument panel.

"According to the garage," Purbright said at last, "your registered mileage yesterday afternoon was seven thousand two hundred and four." He glanced again at the dashboard. "Today you have on the clock seven thousand two hundred and twenty-five." He shifted aside a little and turned his head. "Would you care to check that, sir?"

Palgrove said nothing. He did not move.

"I make it twenty-one miles, since the car was serviced yesterday. And Leicester is—what, eighty miles from here? A return trip of a hundred and sixty?"

Palgrove shrugged and stepped away from the car. The inspector got out.

"Don't you think, sir, that it might be as well if you called your solicitor before we do any more talking?"

II

FROM a barmaid's bed rose Mr. Hive. He went to the window and gently, with one finger, parted the flowered cotton curtains, already bright with sun. Below him in Eastgate the morning citizens passed and met and hailed and gossiped in their twos and threes. Shop boys, slick-haired to start the day, punted forth blinds with long poles. Crates of vegetables, rows of loaves on wide wooden trays, square anonymous cartons, beef flanks and sides of bacon were ferried into doorways from parked farm trucks and high-roofed vans. A girl in a white coat too big for her stretched tip-toe from the top of a stool to clean the window of her grocer employer; she scrubbed away with short, vigorous arms while the grocer, a dim image behind the glass, kept supervisory watch upon her legs. A few women with shopping bags moved purposefully from window to window, pricing, judging, rejecting. Two old men in long, shroudlike overcoats inclined together to examine a piece of newspaper. A crying child's face, wet scarlet disk with a big hole in the middle, appeared and disappeared among the legs and baskets.

Mr. Hive let the curtain close. He poured out half a glass

129

of water from the carafe on the marble-topped washstand and stood drinking it in small sips with his eyes closed as if it were acrid medicine. With his free hand he reached around and scratched the small of his back, the hem of his long nightshirt rising and falling.

He heard behind him the shift and resettling of a warm-nested body, a sniff and a sigh and a yawn. He glanced over his shoulder. Above a ridge of bedclothes, rumpled hair and one interested eye.

"Morty . . ."

"My love?"

"Those women with titles you were telling me about— did they wear nighties or pajamas?"

"I think you may take it that nightdresses are favored by the aristocracy as a rule. The exception I always remember was a Lady Beryl somebody-or-other from Winchester way —we managed to scrape her in at the tail end of the 1935 season—and she, believe it or not, insisted on going to bed in a polo jersey."

"I'll bet that tickled!"

Mr. Hive shrugged good-naturedly. "Every profession has its little irritations. I've been very lucky. There was only one thing I was always particular about: I wouldn't take a client while she had a cold."

"What, like dentists won't?"

"It may sound a rather trivial prejudice, but I think I owe my very good health to it." Hive glanced aside at the dressing-table mirror and straightened his stance. Part of his paunch went somewhere else.

Another rustle from the bed. "Jewels . . . Did they wear lots of jewels, Morty?"

Still looking at the mirror, Mr. Hive preened with arched fingers his wavy, silver-gray hair. "I have awakened in the night, dear girl, with enough emeralds up my

130

nose to pay the entire hotel staff double wages for a year!"

The humped bedclothes reared, subsided and squirmed into another shape. Hair and eye had disappeared. As from far off, a muffled giggle.

Mr. Hive considered for a moment more his own reflection. He pouted, put down the almost empty glass, held a fingertip to his wrist, nodded judiciously, gave his nightshirt a hitch, and marched, like a monk to matins, back to bed.

In the street below, an aging, boxlike sedan was being steered by a fat policeman past the parked vans and trucks. Flaxborough's ancient coroner glared and champed in the seat beside him. The policeman, in consideration for the life of a hypothetical child, rammed two hundred and twenty pounds against the brake pedal. "Sorry, sir, but I did tell you to sit behind." The car moved forward again. Mr. Amblesby, indestructible, clawed himself back onto his seat.

Already assembled in the little courtroom when Malley and the coroner arrived were Inspector Purbright, Sergeant Love, Doctor Fergusson, Mr. Justin Scorpe and Mr. Scorpe's client, Mr. Palgrove. Also present—but only just, for he seemed to be loitering peripherally and without concern— was the chief constable. Mr. Chubb very seldom attended inquests, but Purbright had hinted to him that in the circumstances of this one, it would be as well for him to show the flag.

Last to put in an appearance was the chief reporter of the Flaxborough *Citizen*. Mr. Prile looked as if he had been roused from a twenty years' sleep especially for the occasion. As he sat down behind the rickety little table reserved for the press, dust puffed from creases and crevices in his raincoat.

131

Sergeant Malley shepherded the proceedings along as smartly as the crotchety obtuseness of Mr. Amblesby would allow. The convention was observed of letting the doctor give his evidence first "so that you can get away," as Malley invariably explained—rather as though he were offering a sporting chance to a fugitive.

Fergusson read rapidly from his postmortem report an elaboration of what he had told Purbright over the telephone. He was emphatic about the sound state of Mrs. Palgrove's health that the examination had revealed and described in considerable detail the bruises on the legs and abdomen.

"Would everything you have found, Doctor," Purbright asked, "be consistent with this woman's having been held forcibly by her ankles—held upside down, that is?"

"Yes. Rather in the way one tips up a wheelbarrow to empty it."

Mr. Scorpe looked with heavy scorn over the top of his spectacles at no one in particular. "Is Doctor Fergusson here as a medical witness or as a gardening expert?"

"I see no harm in offering an illustration in language that people can understand," retorted the doctor. He added, before Purbright could head him off: "But of course, I am not a member of the legal profession."

The coroner turned upon him his agate eye; dentures clacked menacingly.

"Thank you, Doctor," said Purbright. Fergusson stacked his papers, rose and started to make his way out. Malley leaned to Mr. Amblesby's long, whiskery ear. "The doctor's fee, sir . . ." The old man remained hunched in stubborn immobility. He watched the door close behind Fergusson and craftily smiled to himself. "Eh?" he said.

Purbright led Palgrove through his brief, formal evidence of identification; then Sergeant Malley quietly laid a typewritten slip on the table before the coroner. Mr. Amblesby lowered his gaze.

"I now adjourn this inquiry sine die—to enable the police to—to make further investigations."

All but Mr. Amblesby rose. He stared at them suspiciously for several seconds. Malley touched his arm. "You said you wanted some sausage on the way back, sir. I'll stop at Spain's if you come along now." Grudgingly the old man stood up. Malley ushered him out.

"I do believe he's gotten even worse," said Mr. Chubb. It was five minutes later, and the chief constable and Purbright were on their own in the room.

"You think so, sir?"

"Well, don't *you*, Mr. Purbright? You see more of him than I do."

"Malley says he's a wonderful old gentleman for his age."

"Does he, indeed? I must say I admire the way Mr. Malley seems to manage him."

"Oh, like a mother, sir. I don't know what would happen to poor old Mr. Amblesby if it weren't for the sergeant."

The chief constable pondered Malley's devotion, then dismissed the subject with a satisfied nod. "Now, then, Mr. Purbright," he said briskly, "what have you got to tell me about this unfortunate lady from Brompton Gardens?"

The inspector, too, became more businesslike in manner.

"At the moment, everything points to the husband. He's given a hopelessly unsatisfactory account of himself—two accounts, in fact: one disproved and the other unlikely. There's not much material evidence, but that wasn't to be expected, anyway. What there is, he can't even begin to explain. His cigarette case in the water under the body, for instance. And those letters she sent to people. There's no doubt at all that she wrote them."

"Where does he say he was at the time when his wife was drowned?"

"At first he said he'd been to Leicester that night and had slept in his car after stopping on the road home. Unluckily for him, the car had just been serviced, and the mileage recorded on the service log made nonsense of his story. He didn't even try and bluster it out. He changed it altogether."

"And do you believe the second story?"

"I accept it because it cannot be disproved, sir. Not on what evidence we have. And if he's still lying, the odd thing about this second tale is that it does him no good at all.

"The Palgroves bought themselves a cottage a couple of years ago, you see, sir. It's a few miles out along the Brocklestone road. At Hambourne Dyke. They used to spend weekends there, but the novelty eventually wore off, and they went more and more rarely. What Palgrove now says is that he stayed in that cottage during the whole of the night of his wife's death."

"What reason did he give for that?"

"He said he needed to be on his own occasionally. He denied ever quarreling seriously with his wife but said she had a forceful personality that was liable to get on his nerves. That night just happened to be one when he felt this compulsion to have a spell of solitude."

Mr. Chubb considered. "It does sound reasonable, you know, Mr. Purbright."

"On the face of it, yes. So why the tale about going to Leicester? Which, incidentally, he'd told in advance to his secretary at the factory."

"Oh, I think that's easily enough explained. It was the excuse he'd prepared for his wife. No woman likes to think that her husband is spending a night away from home simply because he wants a rest from her."

134

Purbright's brow lifted slightly. "Oh, I see, sir. I'm afraid that wouldn't have occurred to me."

Mr. Chubb looked uncomfortable.

"There is something else I ought to mention," Purbright went on. "The suggestion is strong that Palgrove has for some time been having an affair with a married woman. This would be a much more cogent reason for his going out to the cottage than a sudden desire for solitude. He doesn't strike me as the contemplative type."

"Do you know who the woman is?"

"Not yet, sir. But I expect to, shortly. Sergeant Love is very resourceful in these matters."

"I suppose you can't afford to be oversqueamish in a case like this."

"No, sir, you can't."

Mr. Chubb frowned. "It seems such a pity that these people spoil things for themselves—and for others, too, of course." He paused, looked up. "What do you propose to ask the lady when you find her—or when Mr. Love finds her, rather?"

"The situation will be somewhat delicate. . . ."

"It will, indeed."

"No, sir, I didn't mean in a moral sense. Delicate in a criminal sense. You see, Palgrove may be denying the existence of a mistress—as he persisted in doing yesterday, by the way—not because he simply wants to protect her reputation but because she was an accomplice in the murder of his wife." The inspector watched Mr. Chubb's face. "You remember, of course, what Mrs. Palgrove wrote in her letter?"

"Something about a plot, a plan . . ."

"Precisely, sir. *I have heard the plan discussed.* If murder was being proposed—as she very plainly stated—who else but the mistress would be the second party to the conversa-

135

tion? It may very well be that Palgrove was, as he says, at the cottage that night. The woman, too. But he needed only to make a ten-minute car trip to kill his wife. He could have been back again in half an hour. And we needn't expect the mistress to do other than swear that Palgrove never left the cottage at all."

The chief constable said he saw how difficult the situation might prove. Had the inspector any other lines of inquiry in mind? Yes, said Purbright, he had, but he entertained no great hopes of them. Mr. Chubb was sorry to hear that, but he was sure something would emerge sooner or later that would repay his trouble.

"There was one thing Palgrove said that I'm inclined to believe," Purbright announced, rather as an afterthought. "He claimed that somebody had been following him about a good deal lately. A stranger."

"Doesn't that sound a little fanciful?"

"That is what I thought at first. But he described the man in some detail, and I think I know who he is."

"Not a local man, you say?"

"No, sir. A Londoner. A man who follows—or followed once—a somewhat odd profession."

"You intrigue me, Mr. Purbright."

"Mr. Hive is an intriguing character. I happened to—"

"Hive—is that his name?"

"Yes, sir. Mortimer Hive. As I was saying, I happened to see him yesterday morning. He was going into the office of those Charity Alliance people in Saint Anne's Gate. And it was to them, by curious coincidence, that Mrs. Palgrove had sent the day before a remarkably acrimonious letter."

"Good gracious," said the chief constable, feeling that to sound surprised was better than to confess the absolute bafflement he really felt.

"So I think I shall try and chase Mr. Hive up and see what he can tell us. Don't you agree, sir?"

Mr. Chubb looked at the ceiling. "On balance, I, ah, . . . yes. Oh, yes."

12

"AM I, by happy fortune, speaking to Dover?" Mr. Hive inquired sweetly into the telephone at the back of a dowdy little newsagent's shop in Station Road.

He heard a snort of exasperation, followed by a click and the deadening of the line.

Amiably he inserted more money and dialed again. After a fairly long interval came a curt, impatient "Hello."

"Dover?" cooed Mr. Hive. "Hastings here."

"I thought you were going back to London."

"The gentleman here at the shop says that you have not yet collected my account. I know it's rather—"

"I said, I thought you were going back to London." The voice was suppressed but urgent, angry.

"Ah, but events have conspired—very pleasantly conspired, I may say—to delay my passage. That is what I—"

"I am not interested in your private odysseys. I employed you to do a specific job, and that job is now finished. I did *not* employ you to pester and embarrass me. Is that clear?"

Hive's euphoria was proof against rebuke even as sharp

138

as this. He listened as though to a transmission of birthday greetings, then nodded delightedly.

"*Mais oui, mon capitaine,* you are absolutely right. I say, isn't it rather nice to be talking without all those trade terms? No wonder most detectives are bad conversationalists—"

"Are you leaving today?"

"I was just going to say that this good fellow at the shop—"

"I said, *are you leaving today?* Are—you—returning—to London—today?"

"I rather doubt it, actually. Events have conspired—"

"When *are* you going?"

Hive sighed. "All too soon, I fear."

"Tomorrow?"

"And tomorrow and tomorrow and tomorrow," dreamily crooned Mr. Hive.

"Now look, I want a straight answer. And I don't advise you to waste any more of my time."

"No. Quite. Now how can I best reply to your esteemed inquiry? Perhaps I should say that I have acquired commitments. Nonprofessional, let it be understood, *amigo mio.* And in no sense undesirable. But as I say, this good fellow at the shop tells me that my account (plain wrapped, *ça va sans dire*) is uncollected, therefore undischarged. I do not complain. Rather do I respectfully petition. You catch, perhaps, my drift?"

"You want your money at once. On the nail. Like a cats'-meat man or something."

"Cats'-meat—no, I'm afraid that allusion defeats me. Sauce for ganders, I would have thought, was the commodity in—"

"Twelve pounds. On account. I can leave twelve pounds

139

for you at the shop at about a quarter past four. Not before."

"That would be a most welcome accommodation. It really would." Hive eased himself from the wall against which he had been leaning and with his free hand adjusted the hang of his jacket.

"In return, I want a definite undertaking from you."

"Yours ever to serve, *mon général!*"

"I shall leave you that money on condition that you are to leave Flaxborough tomorrow. The rest I'll mail on to you. But you are to be away from the town tomorrow. Is that clearly understood?"

Hive hesitated.

"I said, is that understood?"

"I understand what you want, yes. But I really cannot see why—"

"Do you want this money, or don't you?"

"Oh, certainly I do."

"Very well, then. You will be on your way back to London in the morning?"

"That is my inal—inalienable intention."

On his way out of the shop, Hive paused to speak to a vast, pear-shaped man wedged between the counter and a tier of shelves filled with packets of cigarettes and cans of tobacco.

"A gentleman will be calling later today to leave a letter for me. My name is Mr. Hastings. Oh, and you might remind him to be sure and take that envelope I gave you yesterday."

The pear-shaped man compressed some of his chins so as to produce a grunt and a nod at the same time.

On the other side of the town, Inspector Purbright was in search of the secretary of the Flaxborough and Eastern

140

Counties Charities Alliance. He had called at the office in St. Anne's Gate to find it in the charge of a lady wearing rimless spectacles and a blue felt hat of the shape, size, and for all he knew, the durability of an army field helmet. She had smiled terribly upon him and explained that this was Miss Teatime's afternoon "on" at Old Hall and that he had better hie him thither at once if he wanted to have a word with her before the arrival of the Hobbies and Needlework Subcommittee.

At the hall, a big, early-Georgian manor house set in parkland on the southern outskirts of Flaxborough, Purbright was directed to the number-two recreation room. It was at the end of a long, stone-flagged corridor lined on one side with windows on whose white-painted sills were great quantities of summer flowers in terra-cotta pots and bowls. Mixed with the scent of the flowers were smells of plasticine and paintboxes and rubber boots and small children's clothes. Some twenty coats and hats hung on a row of hooks outside the room that had been pointed out to the inspector. Behind its door a lot of noise was being produced. It sounded like very happy noise.

The door opened. Purbright stepped quickly into its lee as a wave of children burst through. The hats and coats were tossed and tugged and waved and trampled but eventually were sorted and appropriated and trotted off in. The corridor emptied.

Purbright peeped through the door. He saw Miss Teatime at once. She was sitting, erect but genial, in a large spindle-back chair. Around the chair were scattered the cushions and stools on which Purbright supposed the children had been sitting to hear her tell a story.

There were other people in the room: three plump young women in some kind of nurse's uniform, two older but jolly-faced women—housemothers, did they call them?

141

—and a formidable lady in an apron, long skirt and button boots who scratched her bottom a great deal and kept laughing in a bartender's bass-baritone; it seemed that she was the cook of the establishment.

"What about one for us, duckie?" the cook called out.

"Yes, do!"

"Go on, Miss T!"

Miss Teatime smiled demurely and gazed out of the window for inspiration. Purbright sidled into the room, closing the door quietly behind him. No one noticed his arrival.

"Very well," said Miss Teatime. She folded her hands in her lap. "This is a story of the mysterious Orient. It was told me by my uncle—the missionary one, you remember —and I venture to think that you will find it as strange a tale as any to have come out of those fascinating lands.

"It concerns a poor Arab by the name of Mamoud. One day, this Arab was crossing the great Gobi Desert. He was too poor to own a camel, and so he was making the journey on foot.

"Now perhaps I should explain that the place in the desert where these extraordinary events occurred was many miles from any human settlement, many miles indeed from the nearest oasis.

"Anyway, there was Mamoud, patiently making his way over the endless dunes and thinking perhaps of the cup of refreshing sherbet that awaited him at journey's end in some shady Casbah, when suddenly his big toe struck against an object in the sand. The Arab stopped and bent down, groping about in the sand where he had last put his foot. He drew something out. And do you know what it was?"

Miss Teatime paused and looked from one to another of her audience. In silence they shook their heads.

"A cricket ball!

"Poor Mamoud stared in wonder. *Allah caravanserie baksheesh!* And he went on his way.

"But he had not traveled very much farther when he received in the big toe of his other foot a sensation exactly the same as before. He stopped. He bent down. He groped about. And again he drew something from the sand. Yes . . . another cricket ball! He stared in even greater wonder. *Allah caravanserie baksheeshbakar!* And the Arab continued upon his journey.

"But he had not taken more than another twenty paces when yet again his foot encountered an object hidden in the sand. He stopped. He bent down. He groped about. He drew something from the sand. . . ."

Miss Teatime leaned forward a fraction. She raised her brows questioningly at her audience.

"Another cricket ball?" offered the youngest of the nurses.

"Oh, no . . ." Miss Teatime sat back again in her chair. "A castrated cricket."

Purbright waited until the cook, the nurses and the housemothers had gone about their duties. Then he rose and crossed the room to where Miss Teatime was now seated at a table in the window bay, preparing to stitch a rent in a limp and grubby teddy bear. She looked up.

"Why, Inspector! How very nice to see you!"

Purbright took her extended hand and made a short bow. He drew up another chair to the table and sat facing her.

"I'm told you are liable to be swooped upon by some committee or other"—he saw her wince resignedly—"so I'll be very policemanlike and come straight to the point."

"By all means." Miss Teatime drew a length of cotton

143

from a reel, snapped it expertly and at the second attempt piloted its end into her needle.

"Perhaps you have heard already of the death of Mrs. Henrietta Palgrove. She was drowned the night before last in the garden of her home."

"I did know, yes. A shocking affair. It has been quite widely discussed, of course."

"I imagine so. She would be well known among social workers, committee members—people like that."

"Certainly." Miss Teatime pierced the teddy bear's threadbare hide with the needle. "She was an exceptionally active lady, was Mrs. Palgrove."

"It might be argued," said Purbright, "that active people are more liable to make enemies than the passive ones. Or would it be wildly unreasonable to expect this to apply in the field of good works?"

Miss Teatime raised a shrewd eye from her work. "I think you know as well as I do, Inspector, that there is no more fertile soil for the burgeoning of homicide."

"You shock me, Miss Teatime."

"Oh, no, I do not. You would not be here now if your thoughts had not been following the same line."

"You mustn't make too much of this. The person who killed Mrs. Palgrove is very clearly indicated by the evidence. I've no doubt that that person will be arrested and charged quite soon. But every other possibility must be examined thoroughly in the meantime."

Miss Teatime drew taut the thread of another stitch. "And am I one of the other possibilities, Inspector?" She was smiling.

"You received a letter yesterday from Mrs. Palgrove."

"That is correct. Have you read it? Oh, yes, you must have done. I suppose a copy was in what I believe are called the effects of the deceased."

144

It was a very threatening letter, Miss Teatime."

She shrugged lightly. "I can see that you are not accustomed to handling the correspondence of charitable societies, Mr. Purbright. If one took seriously every hint of nefarious goings-on, one would have no time left for the collection of funds. And what would our animals do then, poor things?"

"There is no truth, I take it, in the suggestion that there has been misappropriation of funds."

"None, of course. It is misapprehension, not misappropriation, that bedevils the work of charities. People do not realize how high is the cost of administration nowadays. Modern conditions demand the employment of all sorts of expensive devices—promotion campaigns, the public relations consultant, accountants, the business efficiency expert, even computers. My goodness, Inspector, there is a great deal more to it than waving a collecting box. Which" —she raised a finger and smiled sweetly—"reminds me . . ."

She put the teddy bear aside and went to the fireplace, on the mantel of which was a box. She brought the box back and set it between them. "Just my little charge for allowing you to interview me."

Purbright grinned and found some coins to drop in the box.

"Purely as a formality, Miss Teatime—you do understand that?—could you just tell me where you were on the night of the twelfth—the night before last, that is? From ten o'clock onward, say."

Her eyes widened. "In bed, Inspector. Where else?"

He smiled. "It clearly would be impertinent of me to ask of whom I might seek corroboration of that."

"Not in the least. I should take it as a compliment." Her gaze saddened a little and fell. "But no, I have left things

145

rather late. To tell the truth, it is regarding the physical side of marriage that I have always been apprehensive."

He nodded sympathetically.

"There so seldom seems to be enough of it," said Miss Teatime.

She consulted a small silver dress watch. "Dear me, I fear that committee will be bearing down at any moment. Is there any other matter in which I may try and help you, Inspector?"

His offer of a cigarette having met with a maidenly refusal, Purbright lit one himself and asked:

"Do you happen to be acquainted with a man called Hive?"

"Mortimer? Well, fancy your knowing Mortimer Hive! Oh, yes, we are old friends."

"What does he do, precisely?"

"As a matter of fact, he is in your own line of business, Inspector. Mr. Hive is a detective. A private detective, of course—not on the panel, so to speak."

"He doesn't look much like a detective."

"No? Well, he was not brought up to it, you know. But he had a very distinguished career in what I suppose is an allied calling. He was until fairly recently a groundsman."

"Groundsman?"

She smiled at Purbright's perplexity. "A little joke of his, Inspector. Mr. Hive was a professional co-respondent. He provided grounds for divorce, you know. Of course, you will not let this go any further?"

"Why, is it a secret?"

"Oh, no—not at all. But Mortimer is at that age when men tend to be a little vain and a little touchy about their physique. His close friends are well aware that he retired

146

from business for reasons of health, but I suspect he would feel hurt if the fact were made generally known."

"Do you know why he's here in Flaxborough?"

"That is a question which I think you should address to him in person, Mr. Purbright. The most that I can properly say is that his engagement is connected, as you might imagine, with the infidelity of one of our fellow citizens. Incidentally, I believe the client, as Mortimer would call him, has now terminated it. The engagement, I mean—not the infidelity. Although perhaps that has lapsed as well."

"Can you suggest why Mr. Hive has been keeping the husband of Mrs. Palgrove under observation?"

Miss Teatime shook her head reprovingly. "Now, Inspector!"

"Not even in strict confidence?"

"I really cannot tell you anything more."

Purbright was looking at the collecting box. He touched it casually, shifting it so that he could read the label.

"Tell me—what are the objects of the New World Pony Rescue Campaign?"

Miss Teatime glanced fondly at the box. "Well, perhaps I might describe them as almost missionary in character. Animal-aid work is something that knows no frontiers. And as you well know, in America the horse is man's helpmate on a far greater scale than in a little, highly mechanized country like England."

"Really?"

"Oh, yes. Have you not visited America, Mr. Purbright?"

"I'm afraid not."

"Ah, then you will not be familiar with the plight of our equine friends in such cities as San Francisco. Those cruelly steep hills."

"But surely there are cable cars in San Francisco?"

Miss Teatime regarded him with a mild, patient smile.

"And what, pray, did you suppose was down there under the road, pulling the cable, Inspector?" She allowed him time to grasp the obvious, then sighed. "Oh, yes, there is much yet to be put right by the NWPRC."

Purbright took another look at the collecting box. "It is a registered charity, I suppose? I wonder if you'd mi—"

"Oh, dear!" Miss Teatime had risen and was staring out of the window. "Here come those tiresome committee people. I shall have to go and meet them."

Purbright stood. "Just a moment, Miss Teatime. Your friend, Mr. Hive—"

"You shall meet him, Inspector. This very day. Can you make it convenient to be at my office at a quarter to five?"

"I think so."

She held out her hand. The smile she gave him was friendly, almost affectionate.

13

WHEN Inspector Purbright walked into police headquarters after lunch, he was told that there had been a call for him two hours previously from Nottingham City Police. They would ring him again at two thirty.

He found Sergeant Love awaiting him in his office.

"I've found that tottie for you," Love announced with transparent casualness.

"You sound like a procurer, Sid. What are you talking about?" He sat sideways behind his desk and picked around among the papers that had landed there since morning.

"The tottie Pally Palgrove was fooling around with. I told you before. You said, find out her name."

Purbright, interested, looked up.

"Doreen Booker," Love said. "That's who it is." He looked at the open notebook he had been holding on Purbright's arrival. "Twenty-five Jubilee Park Crescent."

"Booker . . ."

Love watched the inspector stroke his lip thoughtfully with one finger. He hastened to elaborate. "One of the Anderson girls from Harlow Place before she got married.

Used to go around with Mogs Cooper until he piled up that bike of his. You remember—Three Ponds Corner. They reckon Stan Biggadyke over at Chalmsbury got her in trouble at one time, but I doubt if that's right. Anyway, she ended up with that bloke Booker at the grammar school. She's supposed to be still pretty warm in the withers. I wouldn't know about that, though."

"But Mr. Palgrove would, I presume?"

"So I'm told."

"Right, Sid. Thanks very much." Purbright wrote on a jotting pad. "Twenty-five, you said . . ."

"Jubilee Park Crescent. Yes."

Purbright leafed through a telephone directory, picked up his receiver. "Flaxborough four-one-seven-five . . ."

"Mrs. Booker? This is Detective Inspector Purbright, Borough Police. I wonder if you could find a moment this afternoon to come and have a word with me here at the police station. I should be extremely grateful . . . No, nothing wrong. I think you can help me with something I'm looking into. I thought you'd rather come here than have me knocking on your door, so to speak; it is rather a delicate matter . . . Yes, that's fine. Very nice of you."

He rang off. "I only hope you're right, Sid. I'm going to look every kind of a fool if you're not."

"Oh, it's right enough," said Love breezily. "Just you ask her how she likes love in a cottage."

"A cottage at Hambourne Dyke?"

The sergeant stared. "You knew all the time, then?"

"Things get around in this town, you know, Sid. They get around." He relented, smiled. "No, actually it was Palgrove himself who told me about having a place at Hambourne when I saw him that second time. He didn't say anything about your friend Doreen, though."

"Well, he wouldn't, would he?"

The call from Nottingham came through promptly at half past two. It was made by a detective sergeant whose name sounded to Purbright like Gallon or Galleon.

"This murder of yours, sir—"

"Which one?" The query succinctly conveyed the impression that Flaxborough was every whit as civilized as any big city.

"A Mrs. Henrietta Palgrove."

Purbright let three or four seconds go by. "Ah, yes— here we are. . . . Good filing system—murders in alphabetical order—hardly ever overlook one."

"We have some information that you might find useful, sir. The superintendent said that I was to telephone you in case you'd like it followed up."

"That's very good of you."

"A chap called Jobling came in this morning, you see. He's a partner in a photographic firm here in the city. They sell cameras and equipment and do printing and developing as well. Mr. Jobling said that two weeks ago somebody had come into the shop and ordered some copies of two positive prints—twenty of one and three of the other. That was on Saturday, the second of this month.

"Exactly a week later—last Saturday, the ninth—the chap called back to collect his order. Now it seems there had been some sort of a slipup in the processing department. The batch of twenty copies had been done all right, but somebody had mislaid the other photograph, the one from which three prints were supposed to have been run off. Jobling said the chap was fearfully annoyed but—"

"What was the customer's name?" Purbright put in.

"Half a minute . . . Dover. D—o—v—e—r."

"Address?"

"Eighteen Station Road, Flaxborough."

"Right."

"Anyway, he took what they'd done and told the girl that if the other picture turned up, the copies were to be sent to him immediately by mail. It did turn up, but not until yesterday afternoon. A small studio portrait that looked as if it had been taken out of a frame. It was handed over straightaway to one of the process men, and he recognized it as being the same as a picture he'd just seen in an early edition of the *Evening Post* that carried the Palgrove inquest story.

"They told Mr. Jobling and, as I say, he came in today and passed on the facts to us. We've got the photograph, too."

"And what do *you* think of its resemblance to the newspaper picture?" Purbright asked.

"Oh, there's no doubt it's the same woman, sir. We've checked already with the original at the *Post.*"

"Is it too much to hope that somebody knows the identity of the person who was thought worthy of being duplicated twenty times?"

"The superintendent did ask, I believe, sir. Jobling didn't know anything beyond what he'd come in to tell us. And he said that with these copying jobs they don't keep records as they do with their studio work."

Purbright wound up the conversation with thanks and compliments, together with the prophecy that his Sergeant Love would be in Nottingham before nightfall. Sergeant Gallon or Galleon said that that would be very nice.

"You'd better get the next train, Sid. You might just catch these photographic people before they shut up shop."

"What photographic people? Where?"

"I'll explain." And he did. Then he said:

"Two things in particular I want you to do. Try and find out if the counter girl is certain that this Dover person is a man and couldn't have been Mrs. P—as I for one would have assumed. And see if anyone can remember anything at all about the second photograph, the one they made twenty copies of."

"Am I to stay the night?" asked Love without noticeable enthusiasm.

"You shouldn't need to. There's a train back about ten, I believe."

Love opened the door. "I'll have to let my young lady know," he said as he went out.

"Yes, do that." Purbright was long past the stage of feeling guilty whenever Love spoke of breaking to his fiancée the news of extended duty. The "young lady" was now thirty-three, the courtship nine years weathered. It was not really difficult to resist inferring from the sergeant's air of concern that the association would be wrecked on a couple of hours' overtime.

Mrs. Doreen Booker was shown into Purbright's office shortly after three o'clock. He noticed first that she had well-shaped, if substantial, legs; secondly that she was nervous and inclined to breathe shallowly; thirdly that her small, slightly receding chin merged with a soft, blanched throat in a way characteristic of big-breasted women; and fourthly, as she sat down and loosened her pale gray summer coat, that his deduction from chin and throat was amply justified.

Her face was just on the well-fed side of pretty, with a full, rather petulant mouth and eyes that would switch easily from apprehension to boldness, delight to self-pity. She wore beneath the coat a short woolen dress the color of marigolds. It was tight enough for a faint ridge to indicate a ruck in the underlying girdle. Her left hand strayed to the ridge, tried to smoothe it out, then drew the coat across to hide it.

The inspector offered her a cigarette. She took it hesitantly, as if uncertain of police-station proprieties. He came around the desk to light it for her.

"Thank you." They were the first words she had said since coming into the office and listening anxiously and with apparent bewilderment to Purbright's preamble about unfortunate affair, Tuesday night, necessary inquiries, Mr. Leonard Palgrove, strict confidence.

She drew hard on the cigarette, frowning as though at a difficult task. Her protracted expulsion of smoke in a sort of soup-cooling exercise was distinctly audible. Purbright was reminded of Palgrove. He wondered if her gestures were unconsciously imitative.

"You know Mr. Palgrove pretty well, don't you, Mrs. Booker?"

"Sort of. Yes, I suppose so."

"How long have you known him?"

"Not all that long, really. About a year."

"But you are on close terms, intimate terms?" He saw she was trying to get her eyes switched to indignation. "Look, I'm sorry, but we cannot talk usefully until we acknowledge this basic situation. Don't think that I'm bothered about people's notions of what's moral or immoral; I'm not. There isn't time for that sort of nonsense when one's trying to get at facts. Now then, never mind that awful police-court word 'intimate.' You're fond of each other, you like to make love together when the chance offers—that's the situation, isn't it?"

She tip-tongued her lips, staring at the corner of the desk. A nod. Purbright inwardly sighed with relief. Lucky Father Purbright. Not unfrocked yet.

"Had Mr. Palgrove told his wife that he was in love with someone else?"

She looked back at him, alarmed. "Oh, no! I'm sure he didn't."

"Did you ever meet Mrs. Palgrove?"

"Yes, once or twice. She was on some of the same committees as Kingsley."

"Kingsley?"

"My husband. I met her sometimes at garden fetes and bazaars and things like that."

"Was Mr. Palgrove present as well?"

"Only once, I think. Len doesn't like that sort of thing."

"Did you ever telephone Mr. Palgrove at his home?"

She considered while she looked about her, holding her cigarette upright. The inspector pushed an ashtray to the edge of the desk, and she toppled into it the column of ash. "No, I don't think so," she said finally. "Not at his home. We were always very careful."

"You never discussed anything with Mr. Palgrove at any time when his wife might conceivably have overheard? Think very carefully, Mrs. Booker."

She shook her head. "Why are you asking me all this?"

Purbright watched her in silence. The flesh around her mouth made tiny contracting movements.

"Did she—is she supposed—"

"Did she what, Mrs. Booker?"

She looked down at her own hand, clenching the edge of her coat. "Kill herself . . ."

"No, we don't think so."

Her face rose again at once, relieved but still uncertain.

"We believe she was murdered."

The clenched hand went to her mouth, almost like a fist delivering a blow. "Oh, God!" Receding blood left patches of makeup standing out against paper-white skin.

Again, "Oh, God!" From the depths of her throat, almost inaudible.

Purbright leaned forward. He had picked up a pen and was rolling it slowly between thumb and forefinger. Quietly he asked: "How do you suppose it happened, Mrs. Booker?"

She seemed not to hear, but continued to stare at an ink stain in the center of one of the scored and battered panels of the desk.

"You can have no serious doubt as to who was responsible, can you?" The question was put almost soothingly. The woman found that her head was moving in a slow, despairing negative and wondered if she had meant it to.

"Did you know that he might do that? That he intended to?"

A whispered "No" left her.

"But he met you that night, didn't he? He says he came out to the cottage."

"I wasn't there. I couldn't—couldn't get there."

"You'd arranged to meet, though?"

"Yes." She was still bowed, motionless, gazing past the ink stain to some scene in her own mind.

Suddenly she raised her head. "You don't *know* she didn't kill herself. I mean, it's not certain. It can't be. Len would never—"

"I'm sorry, Mrs. Booker. We're absolutely satisfied on that score."

"She was queer. You know—willful, moody. And perhaps she did find out. About me and Len."

"Oh, she did."

She stared at him.

"Mrs. Palgrove wrote a letter two days before she died. She said she knew of a plan to kill her. She said she had actually heard it discussed."

The woman's face was taut and ugly with horror, her eyes huge. "No . . . God, no! She couldn't . . ." An attempted smile of disbelief looked more like an agonized leer. "She was just loopy, off her head!"

"We have the letter. It says what I've told you."

"I don't know anything about it. It's not about me. I wasn't anywhere near on Tuesday night. I was in Nottingham. At a hotel. A friend of mine can tell you. She was with me. Betty Foster. Ask her. Twenty-eight Queen's Road. She'll tell you. Ask my husband. He saw me off at the station. And I've got the hotel bill. Here, wait a minute . . . No, that's right, it's at home. But I'll let you see it. I'll bring it. And I'll see Betty and—"

Purbright, pitying her for the pettiness her fear had brought gushing up, waited for her to finish. Silent at last, she looked shabby and very tired.

He rang the canteen. Two minutes later, one of the cadets entered with a cup of tea. Purbright handed it to Mrs. Booker and gave her another cigarette.

"Have you told your husband?" he asked gently.

Fright sprang again upon her. "You don't have to let him know. Please!"

Purbright shrugged, trying not to regret the question. "You'll have to be prepared for his finding out. It's not altogether in my hands now."

"I see." Thoughtfully she sipped her tea. She thrust her head down and forward to drink, instead of raising the cup to the level of her lips. There was something bovine about her awkwardness. Purbright found himself resisting, for the first time, one of the implications of Mrs. Palgrove's letter. Conspiracy? He seriously doubted if this girl was capable of it. If there had been collusion in the murder, she almost certainly would have had a better story ready. He had been prepared for her to swear out an alibi for

157

her lover. *Oh, but he was with me all night, Inspector—in our little love nest.* That would have made things difficult; English juries were inclined to think that anyone who would go so far as to sacrifice respectability in the witness box was sure to be telling the truth. But Doreen Booker had come up instead with a story—provable, Purbright did not doubt—of an overnight trip to Nottingham. Leonard Palgrove really was out on a limb now. It remained only for the law methodically to saw it through.

Mrs. Booker set down her empty cup on the desk.

"Is it all right for me to speak to Len?"

"I can't prevent your doing so. You are both free agents at the moment."

"But if you're going to arrest him—"

"I've said nothing about arresting anybody, Mrs. Booker."

She looked at once confused and ashamed of being so. Purbright tried to think of something to say that would make sense to her without destroying the fiction of his own insulation. He hated this game he had to play by rules that insisted on his pretending to be merely an umpire. The rules gave him not only protection but power as well—the power to use every trick of legal casuistry and intimidation from the safe balk of official propriety. Oh, to hell . . .

"Look," he said, "keep this to yourself, but the odds are that we'll charge him tomorrow. There are a couple of things we still have to look into, although I doubt if they're going to help Palgrove in any way. That's the position, Mrs. Booker. The only advice I can possibly give you is to keep clear. For the time being, anyway."

When she had gone, the inspector ordered tea for himself. It came in a pint mug with a promptness that betrayed its origin ("well-urned," a visiting barrister once had described it). Purbright set the mug at his elbow, and having spread out Mrs. Palgrove's "Dear Friend" letter, he read it slowly and carefully.

The tarry astringency of his first few mouthfuls of tea was responsible perhaps for his sense that there was something about the letter that he had not noticed during his several previous readings. He tried to decide what it was, to define the reason for his new misgiving. Some phrase out of character? He didn't know enough about the dead woman's character to say. It certainly was a womanly letter inasmuch as its tone was emotional. A tinge, surely, of hysteria—romantic hysteria, if there was such a thing. Nothing to suggest that it was not genuine. Anyway, the forensic boys were quite satisfied that it had been typed on the same machine and by the same person as the other correspondence—indubitably Mrs. Palgrove's—that the house had yielded.

The letter's most impressive feature, of course, was the uncanny accuracy of its forecast. To be drowned *by a loving hand* . . . Well, the poor bitch had been right there. Had Palgrove actually threatened her in those terms? No, not to her face, apparently . . . *They think I do not understand.* Back to the business of complicity. But with whom, if not Doreen Booker? Was the amorous Pally fooling around with another lady? *Injection . . . poison pellet* . . . He certainly was being given plenty of credit for enterprise. A fiend in human form, as Sid Love might say (and doubtless would, sooner or later). Imagine living with the fear of . . .

Suddenly Purbright realized what was odd.

For all its extravagant phrasing, its sensational accusations, the letter somehow failed to carry conviction of real danger. It was too literary, too carefully composed. Even the punctuation was faultless.

It was not the letter of a frightened woman.

14

THE pear-shaped man around whom the little shop in Station Road appeared to have been built showed not the slightest surprise at being visited by a police inspector. This betokened neither ease of conscience nor long practice of dissimulation. He would have remained just as unperturbed if Purbright had been an armed robber, or the Pope, or a lady without any clothes. The truth was that the man was so bulky and his premises so small that the demonstration of any emotion whatsoever on his part would, one felt, have been as rash an act as firing a pistol under an alpine snow pack.

"I am interested in certain photographs," Purbright announced after introducing himself.

"Photographs?" The word was blown back to him over the counter on the man's next suspiration, a whisper carried by a steady breeze. Purbright felt the breeze cease; the man was breathing in. "Never handle—" blew across before the wind dropped once more "—that sort of thing."

The next two breaths arrived empty. Then came, "You should know better," followed by the final installment, "than to ask."

Purbright frowned indignantly, but before he could frame a suitable retort the trans-counter wind sprang up again.

"Here . . ." Something flopped in front of him. "Best I can do."

The inspector glanced down at a young woman of highly unlikely mammary development who ogled him from the cover of *Saucy Pix Mag*.

"We seem to be at cross-purposes," he said sternly to the pear-shaped man. "The inquiries I am making concern an order for three photographic prints that was placed with a Nottingham firm by somebody who gave this address."

"What kind . . . of prints?"

"Not this kind, certainly." Purbright handed back *Saucy Pix*. He thought the man looked just the slightest fraction relieved. "The name given with the order was Dover. I know that's not your name, but I'd like to know who Mr. Dover is and where I can find him."

"Don't think . . . Dover's his real . . . name, mind. . . . Seen him about . . . sometimes, but . . ." The man shook his head gingerly. Purbright felt the tremor of even this small action transmitted through the counter.

"Why should he have given this address?"

"Accommodation . . . address. Pays . . . so much a week."

"He gets letters, then, does he?"

The man seemed not to consider this question worth sending a special airborne reply, so Purbright followed it with: "Anything in for him at the moment?"

The man felt without looking under the counter and drew up an envelope. He hesitated for the space of three breaths, then passed it to the inspector.

161

Purbright opened the envelope. He pulled out two sheets of paper folded together.

"Here, do you—"

Purbright unfolded the sheets, began to read.

"—think you ought—"

Purbright moved the paper to catch a better light.

"—to do that?"

After a while, the inspector looked up. "Do you know a man called Mortimer Hive?"

A negative grunt.

Purbright replaced the sheets of paper in the envelope, which he then put in his pocket.

"Don't worry," he said. "I shall explain to Mr. Dover when I see him that this letter was taken away on my responsibility. If he comes in before I can do so, you'd better refer him to me."

He nodded affably and departed.

In the secretarial office of the Flaxborough and Eastern Counties Charities Alliance, Mr. Hive was making a gloomy pilgrimage from one to another of the pictures on the walls. He held in his hand a teacup from which he took occasional sips, abstractedly and without zest. For a long while he halted before the representation of the child on the steps of the public house. The child's face bore some resemblance to that of the barmaid in the Three Crowns. Mr. Hive sighed and passed on to contemplation of the starving greyhound.

The voice of Miss Teatime, fond but firm, came from behind him. "You really must stop feeling sorry for yourself, Mortimer. There is no need for you to go back to London. It is your own decision entirely."

"I was made to promise," said Mr. Hive pettishly.

"Nonsense. Your commission is over. How can this person now order you out of the town? He sounds like one of those American sheriffs whose ponies are so disgracefully misused."

"I promised, just the same." He squinted closely at the greyhound's eye. "In return for an accommodation."

"You could have asked me to cash a check," said Miss Teatime, reprovingly but not with eagerness. She added, more brightly: "Or perhaps Mr. Purbright would have been able to oblige."

Hive pulled out his presentation watch. "I am not going to see him," he declared.

"Mortimer! We have gone into this already. I have given Mr. Purbright an undertaking, and I do not care to dishonor it. You must at least see what he wants."

"Really, Lucy—a policeman . . ." He moved on to the belabored-donkey picture, as if to identify himself with the victim of Blackbeard's oppression.

"Mr. Purbright is not a policeman in our sense of the word. He is a most charming man and, as I hope and believe, a tactful and realistic one. He has already contributed to my favorite charity."

"I'll bet he doesn't know about Uncle Macnamara," Hive said to the donkey. With his teacup he pledged the beast's health, or what remained of it.

"There is no reason why he should interest himself in our good treasurer. He is far too busy trying to find what happened to poor Mrs. Palgrove to worry about charity registration formalities. And Mr. Purbright, I might add, is not insensible to the attraction of a *quid pro quo*."

Hive turned to face the room. He was frowning. "Mrs. Palgrove . . . Which Mrs. Palgrove?"

"*The* Mrs. Palgrove, naturally."

"Is her husband called Leonard? Owns a factory, or something?"

163

Miss Teatime nodded. "She was drowned, you know. Did you not read about it in the newspapers?"

"How very extraordinary," said Mr. Hive. He came and sat down. "Leonard happens to be my co-respondent—or was going to be, rather."

"The case?"

"Yes."

"Well, well," said Miss Teatime, "what a small world it is!"

"No wonder he wants to see me. This policeman of yours."

"You must be nice to him, mind."

"I haven't said that I would stay."

She smiled. "But you will?"

Mr. Hive brushed the velvet collar of his long, narrow-waisted, mushroom-colored overcoat and wriggled his shoulders a little to square its fit. He paused, then carefully unbuttoned the coat, removed it and hung it meticulously on the back of a chair.

"Very well. Just to be sociable."

He sat down. Miss Teatime fished the whiskey bottle out of the cookie jar and beckoned him to hand her his cup.

In Nottingham it was raining.

Sergeant Love had had the sort of fuss made over him at the city's police headquarters that is usually reserved for a mislaid child. A chair, hot, sweet tea, cheery questions about his home football team, a piece of paper penciled with directions in big, clear writing. He had been quite sorry to leave. His hosts, had he but known, were still wondering anxiously if they should have let him leave. But Sergeant Love did not know this; he was not consciously aware that he remained favored at the age of thirty-six with the

164

face of a clean and equable-natured schoolboy of fourteen.

Despite the rain, for which he had come quite unprepared, Love did not take a taxi to the photographic store. This was partly because he regarded taxi riding as an extravagance of a slightly sinful sort, like crème de menthe and carpeted toilets; partly because he enjoyed looking into shop windows. The walk took him a quarter of an hour and soaked his shoulders, shoes and trouser legs, yet he could have wished it twice as long. It was only when he entered the store to be greeted with "Now, son, what can I do for you?" that his euphoria trickled away with the water from his turned-up collar. As sternly as he could, he corrected the man's underestimate of his age and station and asked to be taken to the manager.

Mr. Jobling was middle-aged and well aware that showing surprise at the youthfulness of policemen was a classic symptom of impending senility, so he kept his thoughts to himself and busily cooperated. He caused to be paraded in turn before the sergeant all three members of the staff who could reasonably be hoped to recollect anything at all about the mysterious Mr. Dover and his photographic requirements.

The first, an overseer with serene eyes and a white-fuzzed dome, proved to have an equally abbotlike desire to assist the visiting traveler. It was more than matched, however, by his seraphic blankness of memory. As this man wandered off, apologizing, Love was reminded of a monastic retreat he once had visited in pursuance of some indecent-exposure inquiries.

Next came the man from the process department who had recognized Mrs. Palgrove's portrait. He was small and craggy-faced and looked shrewd and alert. No, he had not handled the other batch on the order but recalled that about that number of copies—twenty, had the sergeant

165

said?—had been run off the week before. He hadn't noticed the print they'd been taken from. The job had been one of Morgan's, he thought.

Morgan, Mr. Jobling explained to Love, was an employee who had just started a two weeks' holiday in Italy. "Lucky chap," said Love, and all agreed.

That left Miss Jacinda Evanson, counter assistant.

Love smiled at Miss Evanson as soon as she came into Mr. Jobling's little office. Nice, he said to himself. Dinky. She smiled back before lowering her eyes. Love didn't know which he liked better—the smile or the intimation of modesty. In respect for the latter, he postponed indefinitely a certain piece of self-indulgence that the sight of a pretty girl usually induced. He did not mentally snap Miss Evanson's garter. He did, however, continue to watch with pleasure the delicately featured oval of her face, her little-sister shoulders, and hair like a bouquet of gleaming black dahlias.

"Oh, rather," said Miss Evanson. "I remember him, all right. I didn't like him. He was very bossy."

Swine, murmured an interior, pugilistic, Love. "And that's why you remember him, is it?"

"Well, not only that. I remember him because of the picture, partly."

"The picture of the lady?"

"No, the other one. It wasn't a proper photograph, you see. Just a picture cut out of a magazine or something. And I said, 'Well, that one won't copy very well.' And he said, 'Why?' And I said, 'Well, it's not a proper photograph. Look, you can see it's what we call a half-tone reproduction, and it won't copy, not really clear.' And then he said, 'Well, I want it done just the same, and thanks for the lecture, but will you kindly get on with it, miss.' So I said,

166

'Just as you like, then, but don't blame me if they look muzzy.' "

Socko! applauded Love's inner self. "Do you think you could describe the fellow, Miss Evanson?" *"Fellow"— that ought to please her.*

"Well, like I said—bossy. And sarcastic. He was dreadfully rude the second time he came in. You know, when one of the pictures had got lost."

"Yes, but what did he look like?"

The girl considered, frowning. "Well . . ." She gave a shrug. "Nothing much to look at, really. Sort of young middle-aged, not tall, a bit pasty-looking . . . Oh, and pop-eyed—I noticed that. His suit could have done with a press, too."

"Color of eyes?"

"Oh, I don't know. I wasn't all that bothered."

Secretly gladdened, Love wrote down, "Eyes, mud-colored."

He looked up. "Hair?"

"Didn't notice that, either. I'm not sure that he had much." A tiny breeze of amusement was in her voice.

"Hair, thin, mousy," wrote the sergeant. He raised the pencil and casually scratched at his own fertile hairline. "Anything else you can remember?"

She said there wasn't and half rose from her chair.

"Just a minute, Miss Evanson." (*Hirsute Love, not bossy but masterful.*) "There's just this question of the picture, the one he wanted the twenty copies of. Now do you think you could describe the person it showed?"

"Oh, but"—she leaned forward in eagerness to stop him writing down something wrong—"it wasn't a person. It was a dog."

The sergeant blinked. "A what?"

"A dog. A little woolly dog. Begging."

167

15

INSPECTOR PURBRIGHT sipped tea from a cup of the frailest china, patterned with forget-me-nots. At first taste he had fancied there was a curious, faintly spirituous smell about it, but this seemed to have worn off.

"What you have told me," he said to Mr. Hive, sitting opposite, "interests me very much indeed. You are absolutely sure, are you, that the man you now know to be Palgrove did not move from that cottage during the whole time you were watching, from ten thirty onward?"

"Absolutely."

After a somewhat edgy start, Hive's response to Purbright's questions had grown increasingly confident. He was now openly enjoying himself.

Miss Teatime, seated like a referee at the third side of the table, found that no intervention was needed beyond the handing of fresh cups of tea. She was so pleased that her two good friends had taken to each other.

"Didn't he leave the room at all?" asked Purbright.

"Only twice. Presumably to see a man about St. Paul's."

"To . . . ?"

"To have a slash, Inspector," said Miss Teatime in a kindly aside.

"You are quite happy, then, Mr. Hive, that between half past ten that night and three o'clock the following morning, Palgrove could not possibly have paid a visit to his home in Flaxborough."

"Not the slighest chance of it."

Purbright sighed. "There is something to be said for being put under observation by a conscientious private detective, it seems. Mr. Palgrove is a singularly lucky man."

"Do you mean he was going to be arrested for poor Mrs. Palgrove's murder?" Miss Teatime looked shocked.

"That was a possibility."

Miss Teatime reached and patted Hive's arm. "You see, Mortimer? Are you not glad that I dissuaded you from rushing back to London?"

Hive smiled a little sheepishly. The inspector noticed. "Had you made arrangements to return before today?"

"I was going yesterday, as a matter of fact. But there have been so many counter-attractions."

"I trust they will not diminish. I'm going to need you."

"No, no, I must leave tomorrow. I shall be desolate, but I really must."

"Surely a few more hours will not make all that difference, Mr. Hive. You've said yourself that your assignment here came to an end before you expected."

Mr. Hive looked uncomfortable. "I don't wish to appear obstructive, but my first duty is to my client."

"The man who hired you to keep an eye on Palgrove?"

"His wife and Palgrove. Yes."

"But he isn't your client any longer."

"Until he pays up, he is."

"Mortimer very foolishly made this man a promise," in-

169

terposed Miss Teatime. "He undertook to leave Flaxborough not later than tomorrow."

"Do you know why he was anxious for you to go?"

Not liking to admit that he had been so culpably undetectivelike as to have spared the point no thought, Mr. Hive remained silent. Miss Teatime, however, turned a glinting eye to Purbright and said: "But *you* know, Inspector, do you not?"

"I think so," said Purbright quietly.

Miss Teatime looked at Mr. Hive again. "It clearly is your duty, Mortimer, to tell the inspector this man's name."

"Oh, that's all right," Purbright said. "I know his name. It's Booker. Kingsley Booker. He is a master at the grammar school. Indeed, both you and I, Mr. Hive, met him there the other night." He paused. "If you remember."

"I remember very well," said Mr. Hive a trifle huffily. "It was Tuesday—the night I was telling you about. . . ." Suddenly he frowned. "Here—but how do *you* know about Booker?"

"I have spoken with his wife."

"More than I've done," Hive's tone had something about it of the regret of a gamekeeper restricted to a diet of boiled fish.

"Did you ever get your camera back?" Purbright asked.

"I did. Some idiot had hidden it in a cupboard."

"And the car—did you find out who did that?"

Hive shrugged. "I suppose it's just a high-spirited sort of town." He added: "Like Gomorrah."

"No, no, Mr. Hive. As a good detective, you have already decided that these things were not fortuitous. You have seen them as part of a systematic attempt to keep you away from that cottage at Hambourne Dyke."

"Yes, well . . ."

"You have also recognized as belonging to the same scheme the way you were maneuvered that evening of all evenings into taking part in that question-and-answer thing."

By a gesture of good-natured resignation, Mr. Hive conveyed that his cleverness had indeed been found out.

"And then, when you had persisted despite all obstacles in carrying your assignment through, you must have seen your brusque dismissal as a sign of your client's dismay at the frustration of his plans."

"True," said Mr. Hive.

The inspector paused to take another drink of tea and to consider where the flood of hindsight released by Palgrove's elimination was leading him.

He looked up at Miss Teatime. "What do *you* know about Mr. Booker?"

"My impression," she said after some reflection, "is that he is a pedagogue of the rather more obnoxious kind. Even among professional committee sitters, he is noticeably arrogant, prudish, sententious, intolerant and ambitious. His uncharitableness is of the order that ensures rapid preferment in the sphere of social welfare."

"He is an animal lover?"

"That, too."

"But not," Purbright added, "one inclined to sympathize with the objects of the Flaxborough and Eastern Counties Charities Alliance?"

Miss Teatime gave no sign of finding the question mischievous. "He has been very difficult," she said simply.

"With what organizations is he officially connected?"

"The doggy ones, mostly."

"The Four Foot Haven, for instance?"

"He is the vice-chairman."

"So he would be a collaborator of Mrs. Palgrove?"

171

"That is so, Inspector."

There slotted into place in Purbright's mind something that Leonard Palgrove had said—or half said—on being asked to enumerate his wife's regular visitors. *Oh, and a schoolteacher called . . .* Hastily he had altered the description to *something to do with insurance. Can't remember his name.* Naturally not. Mistress' husband. Booker.

He turned to Mr. Hive. "Were you surprised when Mrs. Booker failed to arrive at the cottage on Tuesday night?"

"Very surprised. It was a most elaborately arranged assignation. Really beautifully done. The idea was that she was supposed to be spending the night at Nottingham—but perhaps I told you?"

"That's exactly where she did spend the night."

"Good lord!"

"Her husband saw to it that she was on the train with that friend of hers. He took her to the station."

Hive looked angrily incredulous. Booker's offense against professional ethics plainly was something new in his experience.

"Ah," said Purbright, "I see you've reached the correct inference already. You were employed by Booker for no other purpose than to learn in advance of a specific arrangement by Palgrove and Doreen Booker to spend a night together. Booker knew that he had only to prevent his wife at the last minute from keeping the appointment for Palgrove to be stranded for the night, or for the relevant part of it, with no means of proving that he had not been at home, murdering his wife. Better still, from Booker's voint of view, was the strong likelihood that Palgrove would actually try and provide himself with an alibi for the sake of his respectability—an alibi that was bound to be disproved once a murder investigation got under way. This was a much more cunning ploy than the simple

172

trick of picking up Palgrove's cigarette case from wherever he'd left it in that room and dropping it into the well. Booker is not a man to rely on bits of *ad hoc* embroidery of that kind."

"Now we can see, Mr. Hive, why your perseverance beyond the point at which Booker wanted you to quit was so embarrassing to him."

Hive had been listening with a look of judicious agreement. At the last, however, it was succeeded by a frown.

"You know, what's rather puzzled me right from the beginning," he said, "is why Booker picked on Mrs. P. I've thought a lot about this, but I can't quite see the logic."

"Now, Mortimer," said Miss Teatime, "you must stop hiding your light under a bushel. False modesty does not deceive a shrewd young police inspector as it might me. Admit that you know perfectly well why Mr. Booker behaved as he did. Or am I to guess, and will you say if I am right?"

Hive accepted one of Purbright's cigarettes. "All right, Lucy. You guess."

"I have mentioned already," began Miss Teatime, "that Mr. Booker impresses me as an uncharitable man. That means that he is insensitive and therefore likely to lack consideration for others. I have also said that he is arrogant. With arrogance goes jealousy and a tendency to be vengeful. Someone has stolen his wife—very well, that man must lose his. But as he obviously does not much value her, the account must be balanced by extra payment. What more fitting than conviction of murder—and what more convenient to arrange? The life of some perfectly innocent, if not particularly endearing, woman is an irrelevancy in the reckoning of a gentleman such as Mr. Booker."

Hive glanced at the inspector, who nodded thoughtfully (he was thinking of a certain confiscated radio set).

"Full marks, Lucy," said Hive.

The inspector added his congratulations, which Miss Teatime hastened to say were undeserved as she had merely tried to echo what was in the mind of her good friend Mortimer.

"I wonder," said Purbright, "if you'd care to try another piece of mental divination—you do seem rather good at it —and tell me what you suppose was in Mrs. Palgrove's mind when she wrote this."

He passed to her one of the "Dear Friend" letters.

"Before you read it, I should mention that we are quite satisfied as to its authenticity in spite of its not being signed. So long as it was Palgrove who was assumed to have killed his wife, the letter made perfect sense, even if some of the phrasing is a bit queer. But what now? How on earth was she induced to write such a thing?"

Miss Teatime put on a pair of spectacles. They made her look more benign than ever until one noticed behind the lenses a certain gleam of eager alertness. Purbright was reminded of a village librarian scanning a passage of Henry Miller.

When she had finished, Miss Teatime removed her glasses and looked straight at Purbright. She was smiling.

"Why, Inspector, this is a standard piece of modern public relations technique. In the charity field, of course. I remember that the Canine Rescue League used an almost identical device not very long ago.

"It is a whimsical method of soliciting donations, you see." She tapped the paper with her spectacles. "The letter purports to have been penned by a dog—representative, as it were, of all dogs everywhere that are in danger of being put to sleep to satisfy human convenience. A picture of the beast is appended as a rule in order to sharpen the ap-

174

peal to the emotions. Sometimes there is a paw print at the bottom—very heart-tugging, you must agree."

Purbright tried not to look deflated. "Then that letter had nothing to do with Mrs. Palgrove's death? It was just coincidence that a number of people received it on the same day as she was killed?"

"It is for you to decide that, Inspector. For my own part, I should be inclined to be wary of coincidences."

Purbright thought a while. Then he said: "We shall probably never know for certain, but it is quite conceivable that it was Booker who devised the letter and prevailed upon Mrs. Palgrove to type out copies. These he undertook to mail for her. He could have kept them until the right moment arrived, removed the attached photographs —you'll notice the pinholes, by the way—and then sent them, or some of them, to the people he thought would best serve his purpose. I think it was originally his intention to substitute for the animal photograph a print of a picture of Mrs. Palgrove herself. We know that he ordered three such copies from a Nottingham firm, but something went wrong, and they were not delivered in time."

Miss Teatime was looking at him wonderingly.

"You are being remarkably frank with us, Inspector." The observation was really a question.

"What you mean," said Purbright, "is that I am being remarkably indiscreet. You may be right, but in saying these things to Mr. Hive I prefer to think of myself as confiding in a professional colleague."

Hive smiled at his finger ends and forthwith gave them the treat of a wander over his mustache.

"The point is," the inspector went on, "that I am faced with a considerable difficulty. It is from Mr. Booker that an indiscretion is required, not from me. But how is he

175

going to be persuaded to commit one? What evidence we have against him is in solution, so to speak; it needs one admission from him around which to crystallize."

For several moments, nobody said anything.

Then Mr. Hive cleared his throat. "Suppose . . ."

The others looked at him. His mouth shut again. He shook his head, frowned regretfully.

A little later a fresh thought animated Hive's face. He sat straighter in his chair. "You know, the last time I was talking to that fellow, he practically threatened me. No, damn it, he *did* threaten me. I didn't like it."

Miss Teatime looked anxious. Purbright asked: "What kind of threat did he make?"

"Well, perhaps not a threat in so many words. But his attitude was extremely unpleasant. Guilty conscience, obviously. I wonder, if I were to upset him a bit more . . ."

"Now *do* be careful, Mortimer."

Hive waved away Miss Teatime's caution. He reached for the telephone that stood in the middle of the tea things.

"Just a minute." Half rising, Purbright laid a hand on his arm. "Is there an extension?"

"That is the extension," said Miss Teatime. "The switchboard is in the next room but one as you go away from the staircase. There will be no one there at the moment."

Purbright spoke to Hive. "Give me a few seconds, though I don't expect he'll give anything away over the phone. Try and make an appointment. That will give us time to arrange things." He hurried to the door.

In the other office, he lifted the receiver of the little one-line switchboard and heard Hive's call ringing out. It was answered by a woman. Purbright recognized the voice of Doreen Booker.

"May I speak to Mr. Booker, please?"

"Who is that?"

"Hastings is my name."

"I'm afraid Mr. Booker isn't back yet."

"Are you expecting him shortly?"

"Well, not really. He'll be busy at the school until about seven."

"He's there now, is he?"

"That's right. But I could get him to—"

"I'm in a bit of a hurry, actually, Mrs. Booker. If you could just give me the school number . . ."

Purbright replaced the receiver and waited until he judged the second call to have been put through. On listening again, he heard only the breathing of Mr. Hive and a succession of small, distant noises suggestive of a telephone left off its rest. Nothing else happened for quite a long time. Then he heard hasty footsteps, the closing of a door, the mumble of the picked-up phone.

"Booker here . . ." The voice was guarded, but laden with annoyance.

"Don't hang up. This is extremely important."

A pause.

"Who is that?"

"Hastings—but don't hang up. I've something urgent to tell you."

There was another interval. Purbright could hear faint shouts. They sounded like those of boys. A car engine was being started somewhere. The echoing slam of a distant door.

"Are you listening?"

No reply.

"Dover—I said, are you listening?"

"All right. What is it?" Booker sounded very close to the telephone mouthpiece; he spoke in a kind of curt, lipless murmur.

"Don't you know?" Purbright recognized that Hive was

177

trying to put the right degree of casual menace into his tone, but all too obviously he was no expert.

"The money? It's there. I sent a boy."

"I don't mean the money. I'm talking about Folkestone."

"I—don't think I follow you."

"Folkestone—I know who he is."

"Well?"

"He's a man called Palgrove. His wife—"

"Now look here, Hive, I'm not concerned with this business anymore. It's all forgiven and forgotten. You'll have the rest of your money just as soon as I pick up your account. Or tell me what it is now, if you like, and I'll put a check in the mail tonight."

Purbright waited. Hive seemed to be undecided about what to say.

"Will that suit you?" Booker asked.

"Well, it's eighty-five guineas, actually. There's been quite a lot of—"

"It will be waiting for you when you get back to London tomorrow."

Again Hive hesitated. Purbright swore to himself. The man was hopeless, absolutely hope—

"No."

It was Mr. Hive's voice, suddenly firm and challenging.

"No, I am not going to be paid off like a taxi driver. I consider that you owe me an explanation."

"Of what?"

"Of, of— yes, all right, then—of this wretched woman's murder!"

Purbright gripped the phone close to his ear while he delved urgently with his free hand for paper and pencil. For what seemed a long time after he had found them, there came to him nothing but background sounds from the echoing corridors of the school.

Then the cold, restrained voice of Booker.

"This conversation is becoming a little too foolish to be continued over the telephone. I think you'd better come over here. Straightaway, if you wouldn't mind."

"Hello?" said Mr. Hive several times. There was no answer.

16

ON his return to Miss Teatime's office, Purbright found Mr. Hive in a mood approaching elation.

"Ah, my dear inspector! Did you hear that?" A sweeping gesture indicated the phone. "We are to beard him in his den!"

"I don't wish to discourage you, Mr. Hive, but you must not expect too much from this interview. Booker strikes me as a very circumspect gentleman."

"That is exactly what I have been trying to tell him, Mr. Purbright," said Miss Teatime, who was gathering together the cups and saucers. "He is also very resourceful." She caught the inspector's eye and gave him a private little headshake. Purbright saw that it was meant as an appeal for Mr. Hive's protection.

"One thing must be understood," Purbright said to Mr. Hive. "In your own interests, you must avoid provoking this man too rashly. I shall keep as close to you as I can without arousing his suspicion. If he incriminates himself in my hearing, well and good. But for heaven's sake, don't drive him into making an attack on you or anything like that."

Hive smiled. "My dear chap, this is no time for boasting, but if you think I have never before faced danger you are sadly mistaken. I have collected my fair share of honorable scars, as Lucy here will tell you."

"I will tell the inspector nothing of the sort, Mortimer. Neither bedroom nor barroom wounds qualify for medals in this country, and even those have long since healed in your case. It is only your juvenile exuberance that is undiminished, and I am afraid that it will get you into trouble."

"Heavens above, woman! Would you have me grow old?" Hive threw back his shoulders. "I am a soldier of fortune, and justice"—he glanced winningly at Purbright—"is my new captain! Have I not just given up eighty-five guineas for him?"

Suddenly he looked serious. "Do you suppose the court will recompense me for that? I mean, it is a legitimate fee, you know."

"There's nothing to stop you from suing the estate of a convicted felon, so far as I know," said Purbright.

Hive looked dubious. "It would be rather like kicking a man when he was down, wouldn't it? Those unspeakable, bloody lawyers would get it, anyway." He shrugged and took up his coat from the back of the chair.

As the two men were leaving, Miss Teatime touched Hive's sleeve. She looked at him earnestly.

"Now, Mortimer—none of this Rupert of Hentzau nonsense. You promise?"

Hive closed his eyes and for a moment of self-dedication held his hat against his breast. Then he twirled about and in three long, springing strides reached the door, which Purbright was holding open for him.

They evolved their plan on the way to the school. Hive was to enter first, on his own. From a shop doorway opposite the school gates, Purbright would be able to keep him under observation while he walked up a short driveway and through glass doors into the entrance hall. There he was to wait for Booker. In the hall were the doors of two, perhaps three, small interview rooms, and the inspector thought that one or other of these rooms would almost certainly be Booker's choice for a private talk. The staff room he obviously would avoid, as he would the headmaster's study, and the various offices and storerooms were likely to be locked. Once Purbright had noted through which door Booker had taken his visitor, he would follow and do what he could to hear what was said.

Hive's final eager embellishment of these arrangements was his suggestion that he should pretend to be slightly deaf. "That will make him speak up, you see."

Purbright stood well back in his refuge, a space between the two display windows of a vegetable shop and florist, and watched Hive step jauntily through the school's gateway and up to the main entrance. One of the big plateglass doors swung inward and turned for an instant into a sheet of orange flame as it sent back the reflection of the evening sun.

Remaining all the time within sight, Hive first made a tour of inspection. He looked at some pictures on the walls, glanced at all the doors in turn, and spent some time inspecting a display of pottery docketed with pupils' names on a low table. He sat on a chair, nursed his knee, scratched his head, got up again, stretched. He walked slowly in a circle, head down, hands clasped behind, then took a turn in the opposite direction, head up, hands in pockets.

Where the hell was Booker? Purbright gazed across at as many windows as were within range. The school appeared to have been voided completely. He concentrated on the entrance hall once more.

Five minutes went by. Mr. Hive had settled into a sort of sentry box in the center of the floor. Purbright guessed that he was clashing his foot at the turn in an effort to advertise his presence.

Suddenly he saw him stop and face half left. Someone had come into the hall from the farther end.

The inspector watched intently. Hive was being approached, but by whom it was not yet possible to make out. It certainly did not look like Booker. . . . No, it was a boy. Hive leaned and listened. The boy pointed the way he had come. Hive nodded. The boy went away again, swinging one arm around and around and giving a skip every now and then. As soon as the boy disappeared, Hive turned to face in Purbright's direction and delivered himself of a great pantomimic shrug. Then he began to walk backward, jerking his thumb like a hitchhiker.

Purbright judged from this performance that his guess about one of the interview rooms had been proved awry. Booker had had a different idea.

The inspector broke cover, crossed the road, and cautiously approached the glass doors. He shouldered one open and slipped inside the hall. Of Hive there now was no sign.

Keeping close to the wall on his left, he made his way toward the double doors near which he had last seen the gesticulating Hive. From somewhere beyond them came shouting, faint but unmistakably boisterous, punctuated by sounds of human collision. Boys, thought Purbright. There were still boys in the building.

Carefully he pushed one of the doors far enough back to enable him to peer up and down the corridor onto which it opened. To his left, the corridor was lined with the long glass windows of classrooms. Their partitions, too, were of glass, giving an uninterrupted view to the end of the block.

183

Every room was empty save one in which two aproned women were sweeping the floor.

The right-hand section of corridor was shorter. It went past another empty classroom and then opened into a lobby. Purbright saw beams set with numbered pegs. The noises were louder now. They came from the other side of the lobby. Purbright walked toward it. He could smell the sweat of young males.

As he entered the lobby, there tumbled into it through a doorway on the left three boys locked in a puppylike tussle. They saw him, stopped yelling at one another, and disentangled.

"I wonder," the inspector said, "if you could tell me where I am likely to find Mr. Booker."

The nearest boy tugged at his ravaged clothing and recovered his breath. He looked eager to help. "He might be still in the gym, sir."

"Shall I go and see, sir?"

"Sir—I'll go, sir!"

Purbright raised a dissuading hand. "No, I only want to know where he is. I can find him if you'll tell me which way to go."

There began a competitive babel of instruction. It was quelled partly by Purbright himself, partly by the arrival of an older boy whom he assumed to be a prefect. To him the inspector put his question again.

"He's been taking an afterschool coaching session, sir, but I think another gentleman is with him at the moment."

"That's all right. It's a friend of mine. They're expecting me."

"Well, you just go through here, sir, and along that passage. The gym's at the end of it."

Purbright thanked his helpers and crossed the lobby,
184

hoping that helpfulness would not send any of them in pursuit; eavesdropping was distasteful enough without its being witnessed by small boys.

Fortunately the passage curved sufficiently for its farther half to be out of sight from the lobby. Another feature that Purbright noted with satisfaction was the small observation window in the door of the gymnasium ahead.

He reached the door and listened. He could hear nothing but the noise from the changing room behind him. Warily he peeped through the window. Bringing his eye close to the glass, he angled his head to command a view of one half of the room, then of the other.

The gymnasium was empty.

Purbright went in.

It would not be quite true to say that he felt alarmed. By now, his was the sort of apprehension that is temporarily relieved by each postponement of discovery. But he knew that even in this many-doored building he would reach in the end some place whose entrance and exit were one. That was when mere unease might be turned on the instant to dismay.

He glanced about him. Wall bars, hanging beams, a vaulting horse docile in one corner, a stack of long benches varnished to the color of maple syrup, rolled-up mats, looped ropes and captive rings, windows high out of harm's way . . .

And—of course—a door.

This one was in the center of the opposite wall, recessed between sets of wall bars. It was painted battleship gray.

Very gently, Purbright turned its bright brass handle and leaned a little of his weight against it. The door was locked.

Still leaning, he pressed his ear to the wood.

185

Nothing. No voices, at any rate.

He kept listening, puzzled by a silence that had something curiously vibrant about it, as if it had only just succeeded an explosion or a collapse. It was more like a long-extended echo, sinister yet of unidentifiable origin. And surely there was a sound there, too—liqueous, lapping . . .

Water.

Purbright seized and twisted the handle and shook the door violently. He shouted, banged with foot and fist, then turned and raced back to the changing-room lobby.

Five boys, dressed but still lingering, gazed incredulously at the spectacle of a mature adult at full gallop. Purbright halted in the passage entrance only long enough to take two gasps of breath and to wave the boys into close attendance before launching himself upon the return run.

"Police officer . . . Want your help . . ." he called over his shoulder to the bunch of marveling but game harriers.

They burst in a body into the gymnasium.

Purbright pointed up at one of the suspended beams.

"Any of you know how to get that thing down?"

"I do, sir!"

"Let me, sir!"

The volunteers rushed to unwind ropes from cleats and to pay them out. The beam began to descend. As soon as it was low enough, the inspector shouldered one end from its channel and swung the beam free.

"Down a bit."

When the beam was level with the handle of the gray door, Purbright put up his hand.

"Right—three of you one side, two with me on the other."

Gleefully the boys took up their positions. Divination of

186

what was about to happen swirled in their heads like the fumes of wine. A battering ram! And to smash down a door —a *school* door!

They drew back the beam until it touched the wall bars behind, then braced themselves, half crouching, for the assault.

"Right!" the inspector shouted.

The beam met the door just to the right of its handle with the most satisfying crash the boys had ever heard in their lives. The door went back on its hinges like a flail. A spinning fragment of timber soared over their heads and clattered musically down the wall bars.

Purbright let momentum help him rush forward through the breached doorway. He saw the blue shimmer of submerged tiles and sniffed chlorine.

Ten yards away, close to the right-hand wall of the swimming pool, was what looked like a floating bundle of clothes.

Nearby stood Booker, in shorts and white sweater, leaning forward from his feet and indifferently contemplating Purbright's arrival.

The inspector ran around the pool's edge and lay full length to face the water.

He grabbed the sodden bundle and heaved part of it up and forward.

Boys were kneeling on each side of him, reaching out. Together they pulled and rolled the inert Mr. Hive from the pool.

Purbright spoke to the nearest boy. "Do you think you could make a nine-nine-nine call?"

The boy nodded emphatically and got to his feet.

"Ambulance and police. Quick as you can."

The boy sped off.

187

One of his companions pulled the inspector's sleeve.

"Sir, Mr. Booker knows how to give the kiss of life, sir."

Mr. Hive stirred and gave a weak, strangled cough.

"Hush," Purbright said to the boy. "I think he heard that."

Classic Tales by
the Mistress of Mystery

AGATHA
CHRISTIE